THE PUR
AND
THE PURSUING

AJ Odasso

Printed in the United States of America

Print ISBN: 978-1-953910-87-5
eBook ISBN: 978-1-953910-88-2

Library of Congress Control Number: 2021911763

Published by DartFrog Blue, the traditional publishing imprint of DartFrog Books.

Publisher Information:
DartFrog Books
4697 Main Street
Manchester, VT 05255
www.DartFrogBooks.com

Join the discussion of this book on Bookclubz. Bookclubz is an online management tool for book clubs, available now for Android and iOS and via Bookclubz.com.

A phrase began to beat in my ears with a sort of heady excitement: "There are only the pursued, the pursuing, the busy, and the tired."

—Nick Carraway, *The Great Gatsby*

For my readers, who loved the novella version of this story so much that I couldn't let it rest, and for Baz Luhrmann's cast, whose performances resurrected Fitzgerald's words in my thoughts. As a result, to quote Nick, I'm both busy and tired—but my life has been all the richer for it.

CHAPTER 1

The Pursued and the Pursuing

I think that you will have surmised by now exactly why Jay Gatsby had to die. The matter of what I've written elsewhere is by no means a small one, and I will not attempt to justify it here. Suffice it to say that the intersection of art and expediency left me with very little say in the matter. Until such time as evidence might prove certain parties exonerated or cast blame where most deserved, it seemed wisest to lay Gatsby's ghost to rest.

Even now—in the clear, in this perfect cyclone's eye of a second chance—we've made mistakes both monumental in scope and undeniable in consequence. Presently, I find myself exiled to the greenhouse with a typewriter over the matter of some ill-chosen words. It's swiftly coming on winter, and Boston is no warmer this side of December than Saint Paul. Return with me to the rustle of late summer leaves, to that thinning red spiral ever downward, for it's here that our paths converge in what was once a wood and, irrevocably, meet.

The chauffeur, the butler, the gardener, and I had scarcely got Gatsby across the threshold, his pneumatic mattress serving as a sort of makeshift gurney, when to our astonishment it became clear that there was something resembling life in him yet.

"What's this, old sport?" he muttered, hand slick with blood and chlorine at my wrist.

But for my quick reflexes, we might have dropped him out of sheer shock. I ordered the others to help me lay him aside in the hall and then told the butler to ring for an ambulance. Our burden thus set down, I found myself abruptly the sole keeper of it.

"*Nick*," Gatsby attempted again, undoubtedly finding that lone syllable easiest.

"Now, don't try to talk," I told him, some far corner of my mind beating wildly against panic, and held down his arms as gently as I could. "You've been shot. The man who did it's dead, seems to have done himself in after the fact, so don't trouble yourself with that. You've got to look at me, focus. Help's coming, do you understand?"

Gatsby nodded at me and gave my fingers a faint squeeze, his glaze-eyed expression bordering on the kind of wonder I felt at the mere fact of our disjointed conversation. "But Daisy's not," he said in a moment of diamond clarity, struggling for breath.

"No, Jay," I agreed quietly, although by then he'd lost consciousness. "She's not."

I don't know what kind of miracle got him to Huntington Hospital alive, but I'll sooner credit the ambulance team than my unsteady presence at his tubed, taped, and antiseptic-doused side. They'd cut his ruined bathing suit to shreds. On arrival, I was ushered out of the ambulance after the swarm of paramedics with no small amount of befuddlement; one nurse after another questioned me on the bizarre circumstances of Gatsby's injury in a sweltering hot waiting room, where I spent an uneasy evening and subsequent interminable night with only the dour-faced graveyard shift for company. At some point, I must have slept because it was Owl-Eyes who shook me awake. I blinked at him in abject disbelief.

"They say he's out of danger now, but not by much," Owl-Eyes said. "Poor son-of-a-bitch. Who'd do such a thing to a soul so kind? *Who?*"

Blearily, I inquired as to how the devil he had got there. Apparently, the constant stream of reporters from Gatsby's front gate up to Huntington was all it had taken; he'd turned up for a party and instead found a media circus in full, lurid swing.

"You don't suppose he's got family?" asked the man with owl-eyed glasses. "Parents?"

"Even if they're still alive," I said truthfully, "I'd have no idea where to look."

Owl-Eyes bravely clapped my arm. "Go home. Have a bath and some hot food."

We shared a taxi back to West Egg, in which neither one of us spoke any more.

I staggered past several unfamiliar cars clogging the lane and up my front steps, only to find the Finn cursing indecipherably at a gaggle of men with cameras and notebooks. Pegging me for someone with a far better grasp of English, they crowded around in a greedy clamor for news of Gatsby. Wilson's fate was boringly indisputable.

"What, the man from next door?" I said, at the end of my tether. "He's dead."

They left disappointed, and, once they'd gone, I rang the hospital. Nurses and doctors, perhaps, could be counted upon for a measure of confidentiality, but I didn't doubt that the lower staff denizens could be counted upon to propagate rumors like wildfire.

With Gatsby's privacy assured insofar as it dubiously could be, I collapsed and slept.

On waking fifteen hours later, I found that my Finn had left a cold breakfast tray on the floor and that she had piled several scraps of paper with reporters' contact details beside it. I took the quickest, coldest shower of my life, dressed with an aimless lack of preference, and ate the two savorless hard-boiled eggs on my way out the door. Back at the hospital, in the dull blue waiting room, I found the gardener and the chauffeur seated on two of the wooden chairs. They regarded me contemptuously as if they begrudged me Gatsby's favor.

"Who sent you here?" I demanded, not quite trusting these men of Wolfsheim's the way I'd trusted Gatsby's servants, never mind that they'd helped me haul Gatsby from the pool and get him inside the house. "He's not family," I told them. "He pays you."

"No," the chauffeur corrected me, "it's Boss that pays us. And if Boss says we're to look after his investment for him, why, that's what we do, no questions asked."

"Boss says this 'un is all right," leered the gardener. "Says he's *special*. So fine he'd take him home to meet his own dear mother, even, rest her soul. Let him go in."

"I don't know," said the chauffeur. "I smell a gold digger, and a rather queer one, too, what with how he's always hanging about. Queer as a three-dollar bill, if you ask me."

I walked on by them hastily, damn the consequences, and asked the nurse on duty where they'd put Gatsby. She said she recognized me from the day before as his next-of-kin. She also told me that she didn't trust the two in the waiting room—*or* the shady character with teeth for cuff buttons who'd turned up as accompaniment—as far as she could throw them.

"Your cousin is in here," she said, opening the door in front of which we'd stopped. "This is dreadful," she continued, "but we didn't get his name, what with the rush for surgery. Those men out there tell me one thing, but I'd rather hear it from you."

I hadn't got over my dismay at Gatsby having had a lucid enough moment to claim I was his relative, and part of me supposes that may account for what I said next. "James Gatz," I told her and then went inside without any further hesitation.

Gatsby, gray-faced, was propped up slightly in the monstrous bed, a man comprised more of tubes and gauze than of flesh. I made a start for his side, but the nurse got there first, pushing an impersonal clipboard under his nose. She wrote something on it, and a look of disgust crossed Gatsby's wan features. He flinched from her piercing green gaze and signed. Once the girl in white had taken the clipboard away, he fixed his eyes on me.

"Look here, old sport," he murmured with a weak, ghastly smile. "Why'd you do that?"

"You were James Gatz once, and you can be James Gatz again. Please don't be offended, but you're easily lost in a crowd. Your guests hardly ever recognized you, myself included. I'm trying to save your skin. The newspapers are going crazy."

"*You're* not easily lost," he said bitterly. "No, not you. People pay you attention whether you want it or not. It's something in your eyes. You watch with impunity."

Unsettled, I thought of T.J. Eckleburg and brushed off his belabored earnestness.

"You're in quite a lot of discomfort. I'm sorry, Jay. It must be the painkillers talking."

"It's the second time you've called me that," he wheezed curiously, "in as many days."

"Jay is as fitting a nickname for James as any," I said in my defense but looked away.

"Look, Nick, why don't you sit down?" he said with considerable effort. "Stay a while."

"I won't leave you this time," I promised him and pulled a chair over next to his bed.

"I don't begrudge you the other morning," he said, his hollow eyes drifting shut. "After breakfast, I mean. You had to go to work. Why aren't you there now?"

"Because it's Saturday," I said, hoping to cheer him. His deathlike smile was better than none. "And you're here. Even with the windows open, that house is too empty."

"That reminds me," said Jay—James, whatever he might become— with hesitation. "I need to ask a favor of you, and it won't be pleasant. It's to do with the house."

"I'll look in on it for you, of course. It's no trouble. I'm more than happy to do it."

"It's to do with my things," Jay said, licking his dry lips. "My clothes and such."

"You won't be needing those shirts for a while," I told him. "I wouldn't worry."

"You don't understand," Jay pressed on, voice harsh, exhausted. "It's no longer mine."

By this point, I was certain the drip had him talking nonsense. I took hold of his hand.

"What's not yours? The shirts? Jay, they're yours. From England, bought and paid for."

"The house," he said. "Wolfsheim's to sell it, you see. Couldn't be helped."

A dozen half-heard phone calls between Detroit and New York had taken their toll.

"Oh," I said. "I see. That's . . . well, that's terrible. Of course I'll fetch your things."

Jay nodded faintly and gave my fingers a sharp squeeze, already drifting off to sleep.

"Thanks, old sport," he murmured with delirious gratitude. "Please do. *Nick.*"

I wasn't sure what to make of our newfound first-name basis, but it warmed me in the midst of those cold, cruel ashes that had settled around us.

The green-eyed nurse peered in, her gaze dreamlike through the crack in the door.

I stayed with Gatsby—with *Jay*, I repeated to myself—until Sunday evening. He slept most hours, but in between times, he was alert, if groggy. I read to him from the sad selection of magazines and broadsheets the nurse had brought in from the waiting room. I could tell she felt sorry for us, but I wasn't completely certain as to why. Wolfsheim's people traded shifts out in the waiting room, leaving us more or less to ourselves.

On Monday after work, I enlisted the aid of my Finn in ferrying as many of Gatsby's personal effects to the cottage as space would permit. Wolfsheim's people didn't prevent us from coming and going; it was, as the gardener and Wolfsheim himself had said, that something in my bearing or in my intrinsic quality of character, whatever that *was*, that had got me off the hook. As an afterthought, I went to

Jay's bedroom in order to fetch the heavy gold-plated toilet set, but it was nowhere in evidence. In all likelihood, it had already been sold.

The butler handed me a telegram on my way out and told me I wasn't to come back.

The telegram was from one Henry C. Gatz, an urgent inquiry into his son's condition. He wanted to know if his boy was dying or already dead (the Chicago papers couldn't seem to reach a consensus on this matter), if he ought to come as soon as possible. I took the telegram over to the hospital that night and showed it to Jay. I didn't have the heart to tell him about the toilet set.

"Respond to this for me tomorrow," Jay said, handing the telegram back to me. "Tell him not to trouble himself. Tell him I'll come and see him as soon as I'm well."

"Of course," I said, tucking the piece of paper inside my jacket. "I'll go with you."

Inscrutably, Jay frowned to himself. "I don't know about that. He's not sociable."

"It's not meeting him that interests me," I said, uncertain as to why I found such a weighty confession so effortless. "It's being with you. I said I wouldn't leave."

"I appreciate your dedication, but I couldn't ask you to drop everything for my sake."

An awkward silence hovered between us, but I was determined not to let it settle. "Let's be honest. When they let you out of here, you won't be in any shape for immediate travel. If you'd like to go home in the long run, I'm no one to stop you—" On those words, my throat caught. "But in the meantime you'll have nowhere to go. My place is small, but it's all I can offer. At least stay with me till you're on your feet."

Jay appeared to be considering my proposal and seemed to understand the weight of it.

"I haven't been left penniless. You could find us a better place, nothing extravagant."

Hearing him utter those words, I almost wanted to laugh out loud.

Somehow, I didn't. "There's a second bedroom," I said. "I was originally meant to be renting with another fellow, but he took a job in Washington, D.C. at the last minute. I can't blame him."

"Nick," Jay said, visibly pained, "I appreciate your kindness, but I really don't—"

I left him and went outside for a cigarette, my head full of discordant thoughts. The green-eyed nurse was sitting on a bench, eating her sandwich in the transient light. She nodded to me, and a whorl of red hair escaped her cap. I sat down beside her and lit my cigarette, offering her a spare from Jay's engraved case. She declined.

"You're not his cousin, are you?" she said. "I won't tell anyone. It'll be our secret." Her voice was everything Daisy's was not, and her directness reminded me of Jordan.

"It's difficult to make him see," I said. "He's free now if he'd like to be."

"You remind me of my brother," said the nurse. "He died in the war."

"I was in the war," I replied, after several brooding puffs. "So was Jay."

"We all still are," said the nurse and continued to eat her solitary meal.

I went back inside, past Wolfsheim's flunkies, and found Jay dozing. Pulling the chair closer to his bed, I sat down and leaned with both elbows on the mattress. He looked fragile like that, vulnerable, his heightened sensitivity laid bare for anyone who might wander into the room. I brushed the exposed underside of his wrist with my thumb, followed the tracery of veins up the pale, untanned skin there up to the crook of his elbow. I had wanted to discover for the longest time what it would mean to touch him, and now I knew.

"Hello, old sport," he said, shaking off the thickness of sleep. "Listen, I didn't mean—"

"It's your grand, impossible dream," I said, "or it's me and the rest of your life."

Jay studied my fingers against his pulse-point, eyes suddenly grave and thoughtful.

14

"She won't call again," he said quietly. "I know that now. She's never coming back."

Electric shock; gravity. I held my breath. I couldn't bring myself to look at him directly.

"I admire you because you cling to hope more fiercely than anything, but you can't—"

"But we *can* repeat the past," he insisted. "Just a small piece of it, you understand, in order to pick up where it left off. There are some things we didn't do," he added. "Important things. Grand ones, as you've said. Things we should have done."

Without any further hesitation, then, I raised my head and looked him in the eyes.

"That's not an unreasonable premise, Jay. Where are you suggesting we should start?"

"At your house," he replied. "With the grass uncut and a broken clock on the mantel."

I fell asleep beside him in the chair that night with my hand curled around his arm.

Another week later, miraculously, the doctors said that Jay was doing fine.

"Possible lung trouble later on, though, what with the puncture and the scar tissue now as it heals," one of them muttered to me, "so maybe see to it he lays off tobacco." Something told me he'd take the advice for what it was worth; he drank little enough as it was, so what difference would fewer cigarettes make? They agreed he could go home in a few days.

It was on the second day after this joint pronouncement that a story cropped up in the papers regarding a witness to Myrtle's death who'd never before spoken up. There had certainly been enough of a crowd. The source insisted that a woman had been driving the yellow car and that the man in the passenger seat had been trying to stop her but to no avail.

I read the story to Jay, and we sat exchanging wordless glances in various dialects of melancholy until I finally said, "If they track Daisy and Tom down, it's best we keep out of things. Let justice work, even though it rarely comes for the likes of them."

The nurse bustled in to remove Jay's breakfast tray. "You know who was driving the car? If I were you, I'd pursue it. What's stopping you?"

When I tried to imagine Daisy going to prison, all I could think of was her daughter.

"There's a child," I said absently, and, nodding, the nurse left again.

Jay hadn't spoken since the part of the article recounting millionaire Jay Gatsby's untimely demise at the hands of the victim's husband, of how Myrtle's sister had defended this tragic stranger and for all intents and purposes cleared his name.

"I never knew about that," Jay said, startling me out of my ruminations on the news.

"About Pammy?" I asked. "Neither did I. Not till Daisy mentioned her this summer."

Jay didn't look unhappy about the knowledge anymore. He just looked worn out.

"Can you imagine Tom as a single father? Maybe it would do him some good."

I shook my head vehemently. "There's no fixing somebody like that. I've tried."

Jay sat in silence for a while longer, perhaps wondering who I had tried to fix. If he was thinking clearly, then he'd realize it *was* Tom—and others like him I'd known at Yale.

"Perhaps I ought not to have died," he said at length. "What do you think, old sport?"

"I think death suits you," I told him. "Besides, Jay Gatsby isn't dead to *me*."

The next afternoon, while Jay underwent a final battery of endless diagnostic tests, the Finn and I spent a few hours airing out the house, dusting, and tending to a number of other menial but necessary affairs. The mattress in the spare room needed flipping, and it had never been bestowed with a proper set of bedclothes. I insisted that my own should have a change of linens, too, and if this struck my Finnish housekeeper as incongruous, she didn't mention it. She'd brought three white roses from somewhere and put them in a cut glass carnival vase on the shabby dining room table.

"He like flowers *very* much, yes," she said approvingly to her impromptu handiwork. I didn't have the heart to tell her that hadn't been the point last time, but I supposed that, in his own way, Gatsby must enjoy flowers to have gone to such trouble.

Just as I was getting ready to call a taxi—I had told Jay I'd collect him at five—a high-powered motor roared up in the lane. I peered out the kitchen window just in time to see the red-haired nurse emerge from one of Jay's former cars and help Jay out after her.

The man at the wheel was none other than the dubious chauffeur Wolfsheim had provided. I had expected our green-eyed girl would see Jay to the door, but I watched him cajole her back into the car. The chauffeur drove off into the evening.

I rushed to the front door to open it for him, but Jay, supported by his stylish gilded walking stick, a last gift from Wolfsheim, had already managed to get it open. I took his elbow on the threshold. From the good-natured amusement of his expression, he must have found the gesture preposterous but nonetheless seemed grateful for it.

"Roses?" Jay said, out of breath, but in high spirits. "You shouldn't have."

"What should I have got instead?" I asked. "Tulips? Hyacinths? Jonquils?"

I led him along till we came to the hall. I showed him the tiny bathroom and his own room right beside it. His clothing cramming every drawer and still more neatly folded mounds of it atop the bureau and even on the floor brought a dry smile to his lips.

"Where's your room, old sport?" he asked, jokingly, because, in one step across the hall, we were there. I pushed open the door, and we hovered on the threshold.

Jay leaned on his cane, considering the lace curtains, his lips parted.

"Jordan's a lovely young woman, isn't she?" he said. "You ought to have held onto that one. If not for her, I would never have known."

"Known what?" I ventured, finding his change of subject distasteful. "That Daisy was my second cousin once removed? That I'd be so easily used?"

"That Daisy was your cousin," Jay agreed, genuinely perturbed, "but not the latter, Nick, *never* the latter. I didn't lie about recognizing your face. That was before I had a word with Jordan alone—before she told me who you are. We were in the war."

I nodded, wondering what had prevented me from remembering a glance at *him*. Perhaps he hadn't smiled during the war. If I'd seen him smile, I would've remembered. "I didn't love Jordan," I said defiantly. "I threw her over. What do you make of that?"

"Either you think she's rotten, too," Jay said simply, "or you prefer men." I didn't respond, thinking of my long-distance non-engagement, of the hopeful failure that was Mr. McKee, of the reason for my family's concern when I got back from Europe. "What torture I must have put you through," he sighed, unhappy with himself.

"Don't mock me," I snapped. "Whatever else you do, whatever else you may be, *don't* mock me. Watching it all was bad enough."

At some point during the conversation, I had drifted over to stand beside the bed. I'd been retreating from him progressively, and, progressively, he'd been drawing ever closer. He was standing unbearably close to me now, and I couldn't help but be intensely aware of the fine sheen of sweat that had formed across his forehead, of his hard, tanned body beneath the white flannel suit he'd borrowed from me for homecoming. Much to my surprise, we wore the same size now; he'd dropped some weight during his convalescence.

Unthinking, I reached for his hand and squeezed it.

"Listen here, old sport," he said, lacing his fingers with mine. "There was this chap I knew in France, an English officer. The night before one of our worst engagements, none of us thought we were going to make it out alive. We'd made camp near the Brits. I thought that night would be the end of it, but given we both made it out alive, we caught up some months later at Oxford. He was engaged to marry a Shropshire girl, and I'd received a whole backlog of letters from Daisy." I clasped his hand all the tighter, felt the weight of several worlds lift from us both.

"There was a carpenter's son in one of the villages," I told him. "We made the best of what time we had, and that was longer than most wartime affairs. When the war ended, he begged me to stay. I wrote to my family and said I wasn't coming home. I got a letter back saying my father's health had begun to decline. I left France in a panic, promising I'd come back, and what did I discover in Saint Paul but my father in perfect health and a girl they'd arranged for me to meet. She was sweet enough. I enjoyed talking to her. I wrote her letters for a while even when I moved out here." I sighed. "Rumors got out of hand. We were never engaged, but if my heart had been in it, we *ought* to have been."

"And your young man from the village?" Jay asked with curious, moved intensity.

"My family's disapproval rolled me under," I said, ashamed. "He's married or working or dead, I suppose. Maybe he found another soldier."

Jay swallowed and nodded and then held my hand up between us, about level with his chin. His eyes shone with fear, full of contrite yet hopeful elation.

"Suppose we'd met in the war," he said, "rather than just passed by each other in some victory parade. Suppose there'd been no English officer and no French carpenter's son, no Daisy for me and no family for you. What then?"

"You *know* what then," I said, determined, and reversed the action he'd so bravely begun. I drew his hand up to my mouth, brushing a kiss against it.

We were not perfect, not either one of us, with our boys lost in the war and our girls lost in fathomless expectations up to which we could not live. He was still weak, so divesting him of clothes perforce required care. He sat motionless in his underwear while I undressed for him, eyes shifting restlessly. There was a strange shyness in him as I climbed onto the bed; we kissed for a while before I pushed that brushed cotton down off his hips and pulled him to me.

There was a slowness about our movements that neither of us would have preferred in other circumstances, but even the fever-flushed press of his belly against me was enough. The rain had started up again, a fierce and forgiving deluge, but for me, there was no distraction except for the sounds of our close, quiet coupling in that unassuming bed.

As it turned out, Jay had retained sufficient funds that my notion of traveling till the air had cleared became a reality. We stayed on in the cottage for five or six weeks until the Finn and her distaste for the second bedroom's disuse became unbearable.

Jay was back to his former strength by the time we left for Montréal, although he still winded easily, and he hadn't objected to a reduced smoking regime. We made love in hotel suites on the rue Sainte-Catherine and left for Québec City when we'd exhausted Montréal's charm. There, we walked cobbled streets and spoke horrible French, all the while realizing how much of an impression Europe had left on us both. One night, over *genever* cocktails and a shared cigarette, I asked him if we could afford passage. Possibly, he said.

We left for London the next morning. Going out with a bang, we called it. He showed me Oxford, and then we crossed the Channel and I showed him the village where I'd met the carpenter's son. We stayed longest in the north, traveling from Lille to Honfleur to

Deauville by car, and afterward to Mont Saint-Michel. We lit candles in our turret room and drank cider till the turbulent surf far below our balcony was a fantastical roar in our ears.

We left a month later when our joint finances looked somewhat sobering, and I realized we'd need a place to live. From our departure point of Southampton, we discussed Chicago and ruled it out completely; our families' proximities would prove problematic. New York, too, was out of the question, and although Jay had a lingering fondness for points south, I wanted no part in a society that had in the long run led to such ruin.

"What about Boston?" I said. "You spent some time there, didn't you, as a sailor?"

"I was fond of it," Jay agreed. "If need be, I could turn my hand to sailing again."

"No," I told him. "I'll go back to selling bonds, this time without worrying over you every second of every day. Maybe I'll even prove good at it."

We found a modest townhouse in the heart of Beacon Hill, just above Boston Common. In summer, petals the color of Jay's old suit rain down on us from blossoming trees. I did well in bonds for several months, and then an opportunity at the *Boston Globe* cropped up through a co-worker. In a town smaller than New York, connections were more efficient.

In spite of my attempts to persuade him otherwise, Jay went back to work of a nautical persuasion, but it never takes him far from shore. He turns a deft hand at decorative restoration, has a keen eye for design. I asked if, one day, he'd build *us* a yacht instead of spending all his time on other people's vessels. He'd laughed and told me not to get ahead of myself, to keep scribbling columns till I got famous, and maybe *then* . . .

The past is both behind us and ahead of us, patiently looming, and I am content.

CHAPTER 2

Naming Things

Whatever anecdotes I may previously have related, I confess that scribbling columns for work is the least of my current narrative concerns. My first book about our misadventures in New York afforded me precious little room for *overtly* sentimental reflection. There's freedom in realizing I wrote about our homecoming to Castle Rackrent—Daisy might not have laughed at the jest when I made it, but I laughed at it myself—without blushing my face off.

Since this manuscript has no higher chances of seeing publication than its predecessor, my current reasoning leads me to believe that this is precisely where I should reflect. I once told Jay that if anything were to happen to me, he ought to approach Beacon Press a few streets down, sell the book with our names all changed, and live tidily off the royalties. What kind of modern American journalist would I be, after all, without a scandalous memoir? His response was that surely I'd write some novel or another that would prove *far* more lucrative.

That first morning at the cottage, I woke up with a sore right shoulder and Jay fast asleep against it. He was warm and still had the faintest whiff of antiseptic. I lingered over his hair, let my lips rest against his forehead. I'd known I wanted him, but I had not in truth known I wanted *this*. I must have tightened my hold on him because he stirred.

"Hope you slept all right, old sport," murmured Jay, abashedly, with a stifled yawn.

"Of course I did," I told him cheerfully. "You didn't even kick or hoard the sheets."

When I exhaled into the golden tousle of his hair, Jay didn't so much stiffen as grow tense and press closer, as if trying to conceal himself in what slight shelter I offered. "Forgive me if I . . . " He shook his head. "It's been a few years since . . . with a man, that is."

"It's been just as long for me," I said. "There's little you could say to cause offense."

Jay hid his face against my chest with a sigh. I held him there, my heart hammering.

"Did you always know this about yourself, or was it a shock when you found out?"

"My mother and father knew before I did," I said, "as parents so often do. There was something in the way I interacted with other boys, I'm sure. It's probably why they encouraged me to stay out of sports in school. That suited me fine—but backfired on *them*, as you can imagine. By college, the proclivity had only been furthered by the literature I read."

Jay peered at me curiously. "What sorts of scandalous things *were* you reading?"

"Walt Whitman, for a start," I said, grinning. "Oscar Wilde. Shakespeare's manliest tragedies. You wouldn't believe the hours I spent bereft over Hamlet and Horatio."

Jay gradually abandoned his reserve. "Were you involved with anyone at Yale?"

"Involved, no," I replied, tracing his shoulder blade. "I wasn't brave enough. I had my fair share of fantasies—fixations, you might say. Take Tom, for example. I liked looking at him, but his personality left something to be desired even then."

At that, Jay actually did stiffen, and I instantly regretted having confessed to him.

"I like looking at *you* more," I reassured him. "Almost as much as you like looking at me. I would never have propositioned him, let alone slept with him."

Jay was hard against my belly, trying not to give in to the restlessness of his hips. I caught his lower lip between my teeth, worried at it. I wanted to do everything with him that it was possible to do with another man, some of which I'd never even tried.

"Nick, why did you do it? You had no cause."

"*Hmmm*? Why'd I do what? No cause for—"

"Stay up with me that night. Save my life."

I kissed him, afraid my too-earnest tongue might get carried away. Didn't he understand that being with him was what had transformed the passing of my meaningless hours into something profound? Jay's stomach chose that moment to give an unceremonious growl.

"I'll get up," I said, planting a kiss against his chin. "Make you eggs and toast."

"Not now," he said, voice strained, holding me in place. "Maybe in a while."

Such a distinct thrill of pleasure, being asked to stay in bed. I let my hand slip from his waist down to his thigh, creeping around to the front. He lifted his hips with a groan muffled against the pillow, letting my fingers find purchase in between us.

"I'll take care of everything," I promised, scarcely aware of what words passed my lips as I worked us both into a quiet frenzy. "Take care of *you.*"

Whether it was what I'd said or the fervency of our movements, my fingers and my own sensitized flesh were suddenly slick with evidence of how much he was enjoying the attention. I bit his collarbone and shuddered helplessly under him. We lay gasping against each other's mouths, a cooling and complicated mess until a familiar, energetic string of Finnish and fractured English rattled the front of the house. Each reverberation felt perilous.

"That'll be breakfast," I told Jay, shifting him carefully to one side, and rolled out of bed. "Take all the time you need getting up. I'll intercept the mad old bat."

"Does she have a name?" Jay asked, propped on his elbows to watch as I rubbed my skin as clean as I could with last night's discarded underthings and hastily began to dress.

"Magda," I said, barefoot in wrinkled trousers, shirt half-buttoned, and dashed out.

My Finn was standing on the front porch with a sack of groceries clutched to her chest. She marched past me as soon as I'd got the door open, with only a nod of acknowledgment.

"Good morning," I said, hoping I hadn't left my bedroom door hanging wide open.

"Morning is not good, Mr. Nick," Magda said from the kitchen. "But also not bad."

I went and leaned in the doorway in the event she felt the need to peer down the hall. Magda went about her business from one end of the tiny kitchen to the other, cracking eggs and fetching the skillet, paying me no heed. Her pronouncement felt as if it needed a response.

"Well, that's a relief. I wouldn't insist on you staying otherwise," I said nervously.

"You are busy with care of Mr. Jay," Magda said, occupied at the stove. "Is he—"

"Asleep," I replied, theatrically lowering my voice. "Worn out from yesterday."

Magda glanced at me sidelong. "Only from yesterday?" she questioned flatly.

The color must have drained from my face because I abruptly felt cold. If Magda knew what Jay and I were about, then any amount of defamation in West Egg village might come our way. Frantically, I began running through contingencies—where we might flee with Jay still in such condition, and so forth. The last thing either of us needed was harassment from the law for a reason *other* than the obvious one that we had been so fortunate to elude.

I swallowed and began, "Suppose I were to raise your weekly fee—"

Magda made a cutting motion with the hand not holding a spatula.

"Do not insult me with this. Is not the first time I have seen."

"Ah. That's reassuring. Come to think of it, I'm sure you must—"

"I work for many like you. Mr. Jay, I did not know is like this."

I felt ridiculous for not remembering how many times Magda had brought gossip from the servants next door, *Gatsby's* servants. The ones who had been let go knew full well what had been going on with Daisy's clandestine afternoon visits, so of course, Magda wouldn't have known that Jay had any romantic preferences that were out of the ordinary.

"Many?" I asked, deserving to be whatever kind of fool I must seem.

"They ask for silence," Magda said. "Offer more money. Like you."

Unfairly, I had spent months regarding Magda as less than human, possibly even as something to be possessed. *My Finn this, my Finn that.* Suddenly, I thought of Tom, realizing that my perceptions with regard to class were no less unconscionable than his to race.

"I'm sorry," I said, at a loss for anything else, uncertain of where to start.

A creak in the floorboards cut off whatever response Magda had been about to make. Jay had donned enough clothing for propriety. He stood, watching us, back braced against the wall.

"More money, we can manage," Jay said courteously. "That smells just wonderful."

Realizing there was nothing else to be said, I steered him back toward the bedroom.

If I were any kind of proper writer, I might beg your patience throughout this stretch of seemingly disjointed recollections. In retrospect, it doesn't seem fair to have plied you with hints at our honeymoon tour through Canada and Europe and not be more forthcoming. Taking some time to make this a record of the more salacious details early in our involvement would call for such. I can only hope that the details I've chosen will satisfy the average voyeur.

As I write these words, I half wonder if Jay will ask to read. He didn't ask to read the first book throughout the entirety of the months I labored on it. Perhaps he knew, even in the absence of particular claims or caveats on my part, that I'd needed time to process those wild events we'd so recently put behind us. If fools rush in, as the saying goes, then we've both learned from example and grown more cautious. If Jay should happen upon these pages, I'll beg clemency.

Montréal was an easy first destination to reach by train. Jay spent much of the time in our sleeper car at rest, which begged both of our patience. First-class fare meant the food was tolerable, although it made me realize just how skilled a cook Magda really was. I had the feeling I was in for any number of further lessons in gratitude, although I kept that thought to myself.

On arrival, Jay suggested that we take up lodgings at the Ritz-Carlton. His knowledge of elegant places to stay seemed encyclopedic. With a thrill, I wondered where else his sensibilities might lead us to rest our heads. We spent our first week limited to nearby forays. Gradually, Jay's strength returned to its former vital state. I credited the change of scenery.

The hedonistic offerings of rue Sainte-Catherine proved a fast favorite with both of us. I had heard my father wax nostalgic about beverages more readily available north of the Canadian border, so I wasted no time in sampling as many as I could manage. Jay joined in that endeavor judiciously, which was understandable given his doctors' advice. Even then, he had never drunk as much as the rest of us. That was one of the first things I had ever noticed about him.

Far better for Jay's steady improvement was the menu available in many of the same establishments. Not all of what we ate was unfamiliar to us, although the sheer fact of our long journey lent it an exotic flavor. With each successive meal, color returned to Jay's complexion, which itself increased my own sense of wellbeing. Unease had haunted me from the moment we departed West Egg, even though I knew we might find warmer reception farther afield.

We spent only a week in Montréal, at Jay's insistence that we might find adjacent locales, even the most populous of those, significantly more rustic. The journey to our next agreed port-of-call took most of half a day. The quaint scenery out our train-car window was picturesque, boasting houses with steep roofs that sloped to elegantly upturned ends.

Jay had called ahead to ensure that accommodation was waiting. Like the room we had left behind in Montréal, our third-floor suite in the Château Frontenac had two large beds, one of which we fastidiously ignored. Québec City was unfamiliar but charming to us both.

The *genever* was simultaneously sweeter and sharper than New York gin as it hit the back of my tongue. I set my tumbler back down on the bedside table, my fingers drenched with condensation, and settled in closer against Jay's side. He shivered as I ran a chip of ice down the curve of his neck and let it drop harmlessly into the pillows. It was the first time I'd ever seen Jay something approaching intoxicated. He was enjoying himself.

"We ought to move on," Jay said wistfully. "Before the staff catch on."

"Even if they did," I asked, "would they care? This isn't West Egg."

"No," Jay agreed hesitantly and then fell silent for several minutes.

"We both miss Europe," I slurred, lazily picking up the suspended thread of our conversation. "Lots. We should go back if we can afford it. Do you think we can?"

"Possibly, old sport," he told me, one arm thrown possessively over my side. He delayed any rejoinder on my part with a leisurely, slack-jawed kiss. He showed no hesitation now, two months on. I sucked the gin taste from his tongue with delight.

"Let's go to London first," I implored him, mouthing my way from the hollow of his throat to the still-livid scar on his chest. I lingered there, resting my cheek against the spot. "I miss it. The food isn't as bad as they say, and Regent's Park is magnificent."

"I never went there," Jay said, arching a bit as my hand, well ahead of my mouth, drifted lower. "But I went to Hyde Park and to Saint James's—Nick, what the *devil*—"

I kissed his belly button, his hipbone, and then nuzzled his obvious interest.

"You can take me to Oxford," I said with an experimental lick. "Show me around."

Jay groaned and twisted under me, almost throwing me off task. I held him still.

"Nick—Nick, *look*—it's just that—that's not respectable, you see, not *done*."

I guided his faltering fingers into my hair and drew him back into my mouth. It was an unaccustomed effort, learning the salt-and-skin taste of him, but his movements were captivating, his cries even more so. I pulled off for a moment, catching my breath.

"It's done as long as I say it is," I announced drunkenly. "Also as long as it gets you off."

Jay had gone pale, except for his flushed cheeks. "Even wives and mistresses won't—"

"What makes you think I give a damn about wives and mistresses? I'm neither one, and I want to suck you till you scream. That's settled."

And Jay *did* shout, loudly and brokenly enough to distract me from the urge to spit. Once he'd caught his breath, he coaxed me back up and kissed me as if he tasted nothing amiss, his hand on me as skilled and relentless as I could have wished.

"We'll pack in the morning, old sport," he said later, passing back the cigarette.

The hilarity of that habitual appellation, especially under the circumstances, isn't lost on me. Once, when I asked Jay where in the world he'd picked it up, he asked with shame in his voice if I preferred he didn't use it. I told him that was ridiculous; had I kicked him out of bed for it yet? He agreed that I hadn't, although he also said he wouldn't have blamed me if I had. As for where he'd picked it up, the pervasive influence of Dan Cody was to blame.

This next recollection holds a measure of vulnerability for us both, but more so for Jay than for me. He must know that I'm writing about the days we spent abroad because I spent some time asking him questions on the grounds that I hadn't been sober for most of the trip. His obvious displeasure might have been the knowledge of what level of detail I intended to record—or it might simply have been the self-deprecating reference to my drunkenness.

We were tired of London after a fortnight, longing for someplace quieter. Jay said that Oxford would fit the bill but left the matter of accommodations up to me. Nervous at first, I was convinced that my choice simply wouldn't measure up to Jay's standards. I had an ulterior motive for choosing the Old Parsonage. Jay didn't know until we set foot on the premises.

"Oscar Wilde lodged here for a while," I told Jay, tossing one of our suitcases on the spare bed. "Just think of what he must have done here. What these walls have seen."

"They've seen a great deal more than Wilde and his entanglements," Jay said, sidling up behind me. "They'll continue to witness wonders if I have any say in the matter." He slid one arm around my waist, using his free hand to thumb his way inside my trousers. "Nick," he prompted, inclining his head toward the unoccupied bed. "Leave the bags."

I have always found it impossible to accurately describe the sensation of being the sole focus of Jay's fearsome, miraculous intensity. We were tired from transit, dusty and irritable just off the train, but it was then that he undressed me fully without aid or intervention for the very first time. His own clothing seemed an afterthought, hanging unceremoniously open, as he pushed me down against the cool duvet, sucked me in hard and deep.

When he finally paused for breath and I was near delirious, Jay asked, "Your boy in the war, what was he called? I don't recall if you said his name at the time."

"Arnaud," I told him, fingers unsteady in his hair, against his cheek. "Your officer?"

"John," he said, palming me deftly as he bent his head again. "Nothing remarkable."

"*You're* remarkable," I gasped, holding him down. "Don't let anyone tell you otherwise."

Jay finished me quickly after that. While he did, what I saw against the backs of my ecstatically closed eyelids rivaled his fabled fireworks a myriad times over.

I urged him onto his back and gave him as good as I'd got, or so I hoped. Even as James Gatz, Gatsby was a fast learner and an overachiever next to those who had been in the game for far longer. He lasted so little time that I could only conclude my hopes hadn't been in vain.

Jay studied me as I lay drowsing beside him. His gaze had always had a tactile quality, even in those early days when we'd remained properly attired neighbors. At no point in my younger days had watching and being watched been considered a desirable state of affairs, yet that very reciprocation was one thing I so desperately adored about being with Jay.

When I told him as much, he said, "Watching got me out of where I was."

"Growing up?" I asked, regretting that I considered a luxury something that he had considered a necessity for survival. "I can understand that."

"You're not to feel guilty about it," Jay said firmly. "Your eyes give you away."

Whether Jay had intended that statement to be funny or not, I was laughing before I could think better of it. Everything about the spectacle of Jay's existence in West Egg, and mine by extension, had been prophetic. Watching, being watched, my eyes giving me away . . .

"I don't know how to say this, Nick," Jay began, setting his right hand on my chest.

"Then think it over for a while and say it later," I told him sleepily. "Rest with me."

Resolutely, Jay shook his head, sliding his hand to my hip. "Waiting isn't a wise thing to do. Nearly all my chief regrets are the product of hesitation." That woke me up somewhat and forced me to focus. Jay's eyes were fixed on mine, bright with the effort of holding back tears too long unshed. "Look here, old sport," he said abruptly, clapping my thigh. "I'm yours."

We slept sparingly that night in spite of our travel-induced exhaustion. Come dawn, our sated wonder was the richer for it. I have no doubt Oscar Wilde would have approved.

<hr />

For the first time since beginning this stretch of the narrative, I'm experiencing a moment's hesitation. Jay will forgive me for sharing our trysts, although I can't say for certain if he'll do so as readily for sharing what comes tangled in the one I'm about to recount. No relationship is without its fraught moments, and ours has had more than its fair share even from before we declared ourselves. There's comfort in knowing we've had only ourselves to blame.

We fight seldom but civilly enough if a disagreement presents itself. However, the line between mild discord and cause for heated argument seems finer than before. When I was young, my father frequently made cryptic prognostications regarding the importance of keeping the peace within marriage. Inasmuch as I failed to secure the kind of partner he had in mind, I believe the advice still applies. Nevertheless, I admit to the selfish desire for catharsis.

Saving France for last felt portentous, especially since our last destination before Paris was the fabled Mont Saint-Michel. I gave Jay a literary whistle-stop tour of the location, talking my throat raw as he drove us from Deauville. He enjoyed Geoffrey of Monmouth most.

At Mère Poulard, we had a small balcony overlooking the ocean, and the view was staggering. We'd come back up to the room after an excellent lunch in the dining room and ordered tea service to see us through the restful sunset hours until dinner.

The hotel's matronly founder had apparently been a dab hand at baking; even the circling sea birds seemed to agree. I made some quip about whether or not Magda would agree.

Jay brushed the butter-biscuit crumbs off my chin with his thumb. "Nick Carraway, you're a mess," he chided happily. "An actual mess, old sport. Take it from me." I grinned at him over my tea, hazy from the prodigious amount of champagne we'd had at lunch.

"So what are you going to do about it?" I asked, setting the cup and saucer down.

"Why, make an even bigger mess of you, of course," he said, rising to go inside.

I followed at more of a wobble than a walk, so Jay had to slide an arm around my shoulders and guide me to the bed. They were less prudish here, less inclined to ask questions than Canada would have been. We'd been given a suite with a single canopied king-size.

"Afraid I might not be much use to you," I said sheepishly. "I've had a lot to drink."

"About that," Jay said, patiently stripping me out of my shirt. "What do you say we cut back a bit once this jaunt's over. Just like me and smokes, you see."

"Whatever you want, Jay," I told him, fumbling at the fastenings of his trousers.

"What I want is for you to *last*," he said, laying me flat. "To watch you grow old."

"What, you'll still want me then? When I'm not young and handsome anymore?"

I'd meant it in jest, but something in his demeanor suggested that he was anything *but* joking. He got up and walked over to the balcony door, trousers comically flapping open, and at first, I thought he was going to let me cool my heels and sleep it off.

Instead, he slid the door shut, but not the whole way, leaving enough of a crack to admit the salt-stung breeze. He proceeded to strip down swiftly, sternly, and it was all I could do not to let my head loll to one side and *stare*. Even scarred with old wounds and past cares, he was still the most gorgeous creature I'd ever seen. I tried to tell him as much, but it came out in a jumble that would've made Magda sound coherent at her most Finnish.

"You said you'd take care of everything," Jay said, "but I'd rather take care of you."

"Oh, you've done lots of that," I reassured him. "I'm better kept than Tom's girls."

Jay threw the last of his clothes down and climbed onto me with shocking strength, yanking my chin up so that I'd have no choice but to look at him. Fortunately, he wasn't angry enough to be furious, and I was too drunk to be afraid.

Beneath the champagne's influence, an ache in my chest told me I'd said something careless. "I'm here because you wanted to see Europe again," Jay said. "With me."

"Yes," I agreed, readily nodding. "We're having ourselves a grand time."

"With the last of my fortune," he said, roughly letting go of my chin, and then regretfully converted the gesture into apologetic stroking of my cheek. "I'm sorry, Nick. I'm sorry," he whispered. "I lost my temper. I got carried away."

All I could think of was that it rhymed with Carraway, of how fitting that was.

My changing expression must have conveyed that to him in a series of mute yet painstakingly precise hints because before long, we were clinging to each other and laughing like a pair of Yale undergrads fresh out of exams. I wasn't too drunk to feel relieved.

"You're a dream to keep," Jay said at length, settling between my thighs. "No fuss."

"You give me everything," I told him, pinching his backside. "I've been spoiled rotten."

Jay kissed my neck, lingering a while before lifting his head to breathe hotly in my ear.

"I want you, old sport," he said in a low, hoarse, meaning-laden voice, "very badly."

The implication, however, was that my present performance left something to be desired. I nuzzled his throat and kissed him, reaching between us to guide him down.

"Never mind me," I told him, punch-drunk on love as much as anything. "Do it."

"No, no," Jay said, stroking my hair back as he kissed my forehead. "Later tonight."

"I'm wild about you," I whispered against his cheek, loud enough for him to hear.

We lay like that for the longest time, listening to the roar of the surf over the softer, less obvious accompaniments of pulse and breath relaxed enough to tempt sleep.

"I'll order some matches," Jay murmured. "Imagine this room, this bed, with candles."

"Roses," I replied, close enough to drowsing that even the sea seemed distant.

"Roses," Jay agreed, his voice gone soft and fond. "For you. White ones."

I realize now, only upon rereading what I so foolishly dared to claim as self-indulgence, that there has been deeper utility at work. It was during those dreamlike days and feverish nights that we started naming things in earnest, feeling our way into the implications of commitment. This isn't to say that we wouldn't have gotten there if we'd remained at home. Far from it.

Whether they can afford it or not, men of my father's disposition have long sent young men out into the world as an exercise in developing character. More often than not, tendencies toward excess are what develop instead—at least for those of us with the advantages my father was always so set on reminding me of. Jay sent himself out into the world and, prior to meeting Dan Cody, had no such advantages. Even then, he'd lost them and needed to start anew.

However, what Jay and I *have* always had in common is a brand of survival instinct cultivated under deadly duress. That we should have honed its instincts on the very soil where we first acquired it feels like nothing short of poetic justice—which pains me, seeing as I'm far from anything resembling skilled in the fabrication of verse. Sentences like these would drive anyone to distraction, just as they've surely driven you, my distant nameless reader.

Jay would say that the kind of distraction I'm thinking of and the kind of distraction he's thinking of aren't the same things. And then he'd tell me, with an alarmingly straight face and an alluring glance, that the only distraction worth a damn under the circumstances is his.

CHAPTER 3

In the Meantime, in Between Time

Our return to the United States was not as straightforward as I've previously made it sound. Having decided Boston would be our destination, there was the conundrum of lodgings to consider—which we perhaps unwisely deferred. We had scraped the bottom of Jay's remaining funds to book first-class passage by sea, which resulted in a blissful fortnight spent mostly shut in our stateroom, in spite of various charming heiresses' efforts to draw us out.

Picking up where we'd left off on that champagne-soaked Normandy afternoon, I learned that I liked straddling Jay while he moved under me, watching him fervently unravel. We were two days from port when I turned the tables, feverish with the heat of him, his legs draped over my shoulders. His post-coital kisses, once almost chaste in their devotion, unraveled with him.

When I told Jay that was another item off the checklist, he laughed.

"It saddens me we won't have another night in your old place," he said facetiously, turning so that I could settle behind him with an arm thrown over his waist. "We could've added this to the long list of scandals that Magda has compiled."

"I don't know if she can even read," I said, dotting soundless kisses across his nape.

"The list's in her own language, you see," Jay said. "We have nothing to worry about."

"We have money to worry about," I replied. "Maybe this wasn't a good idea after all."

"Nonsense. We did the right thing and laid low for a while. Now we're fat and happy."

I pinched his belly, which had filled out again, restored to its ever-so-slight softness.

"I sent a wire to my father three days ago," I said. "I told him things hadn't gone so well in New York, reminded him that he'd probably seen all of that fuss in the papers. I apologized for needing to get away for a while. I found an old war buddy in England, as it happens," I continued, right in his ear, "who's been as hard-up as I have. We traveled, paying our respects across France, but we miss home, and we've got it in our heads to share a place in Boston while we find our feet again. We're not sure we can afford it, but we'll make do somehow . . . "

"Your powers of manipulation," Jay said admiringly, twisting his head around so that our mouths touched, "are astonishing, old sport. I must admit I'm proud of you."

We arrived at the Parker House Hotel (which is where I told my father we'd be staying until we found a place, although how we were going to pay for more than a few nights, I had no idea) to find both a reservation and a telegram from my father waiting for us at the concierge.

Renting is preferable, buy if expedient. Come see us soon. Let's meet this fellow. The message was cordial, if terse, and it was a welcome change from my family's reactions to both my abortive attempt to stay in France and my insistence upon moving East.

"They want us to come visit," I told Jay during dinner. "And I do mean both of us."

"Who does?" he asked, hesitating over another forkful of fish. "Friends of yours?"

"My family," I said. "More specifically, my father. He's magnanimous like that."

Jay nodded slowly as he chewed. "Where are they, your family? Who's still living?"

"Both of my parents, plus a whole host of aunts and uncles. Mom has three living sisters and one deceased. Dad's siblings are all alive, two sisters and three brothers."

"They're all in one city?"

"Saint Paul and environs."

"You're an only child?"

"I am. Just like you."

"My mother died some time ago," Jay said pensively, even though I hadn't expected reciprocation. "My father lives not too far from Saint Paul. I bought him a house there."

"It was kind of him to send the telegram while you were laid up. I replied to it like you asked, but he didn't respond. I wondered whether I should've been worried."

"We understand that we're better off the less we see of each other."

"Same with my family and me; although, my father and I have a kind of understanding. We keep to ourselves, but we can communicate when it really matters."

"Then does this telegram mean we're supposed to go house hunting and call him as soon as we've found something? Or is there some hidden meaning that I'm missing?"

"It means he'd prefer we came to visit first," I said. "We'd leave with money."

Jay nodded soberly, chipping what was left of his cod into a neat pile of flakes.

"Then let's go to Saint Paul, maybe spend a day or two in Chicago on our way back."

Jay was unusually quiet that night, turning in early while I rang my father to make our travel arrangements. He was asleep by the time I got off the phone, so I turned out the light, undressed, and climbed into bed as unobtrusively as I could. He didn't turn to face me, but he dragged my hand from his hip up to his heart and held it fast.

My opinion of travel by rail was low prior to our honeymoon. Jay had a stubborn love of it. We avoided the dining car when we could and stuck to our sleeper. Between my brief twice-daily trips to procure food for us both, we passed the time talking and playing cards and, otherwise, being quiet and careful not to leave the linens in an irreparable state.

I knew full well that others before us had been reported for less, and some had even lost their lives, too. While serving staff in Canada and Europe could be counted upon for a measure of discretion, I gave our homegrown stock no such benefit of the doubt. It's just as well that we were in Boston for only three days. We'd used both beds in the suite, one for each night. We'd also made it clear to the concierge that our room wanted no disturbance from housekeeping until after our departure. Even then, I'd been wary and finally admitted as much.

"What about your family?" Jay asked as we rattled over the Minnesota border. "Surely they wouldn't report us. That's what blood is for, isn't it—keeping a lid on a scandal?"

"Little do they know, I'm bringing home a doozy," I said fondly, flicking some ash out the window. I offered Jay what remained of my cigarette, but he declined. "I invited a friend home from Yale one Christmas. He was just that—a friend. Even so, my mother had the housekeeper stick him in the guest room farthest up the hall from mine."

Jay raised his eyebrows. "Your family has more than one guest room, old sport?"

"It's a big house," I said. "We have two guest rooms, my parents' room, and mine."

"Then I'll have to sneak around at night if I'd like to see you at all, is that it?"

"Don't be silly. I'll do the sneaking around. I know which floorboards creak."

We spent the first five days on our best behavior, enduring my mother's cookery and the endless parade of relations with stoic humor. My father took to Jay right from the off, which was unexpected. Usually, I could have counted on him to give the interloper a thorough ribbing. The friend I had asked home for Christmas during college cited that as the reason he'd never return.

Jay's habitual reserve, coupled with a gracious demeanor when he spoke, threw into sudden, vivid relief what Dan Cody must have seen in him those many years ago. My aunts and uncles were charmed by his taciturn modesty. Aunt Meredith, in particular, latched onto Jay, proclaiming him her dashing young war hero. Jay endured her attention with good humor.

"Stay till Christmas," my father said over brandy and cigars on the sixth evening. "It's only two weeks away. It'll make your mother's whole New Year just to have you." Before I could respond—and a good thing, too, since I was tipsy—Jay gracefully cut in.

"Mr. Carraway, I can't tell you how much I would've enjoyed that, but my father's in a town twenty miles from here. Edina, do you know it? He's got nobody to spend the holidays with. I promised him we'd come, but if you can't part with Nick, I'm happy to go myself."

"Nonsense," said my father gruffly. "You ought not to be traveling alone," he added, reflexively patting his own chest. I'd explained the reason for Jay's slight infirmity as the lingering effects of a war wound; nobody had dared to question. "We'll have you driven out a couple of days before the twenty-fourth; how's that? Plenty of time."

Jay was effusive in his thanks, but not to excess. A brief cigar-induced coughing spell provided reason enough for him to retire for the night. My father and I sat puffing and swilling in silence until my father had sufficiently shaped his obnoxious brooding into words.

"Jay's older than you are by a little bit," he said uncomfortably. "Three or four years?"

"Hardly even," I said. "He turned thirty-two a couple of months before I turned thirty."

"You met him in the war? Where? You never mentioned him in your letters home."

"France," I said and then instantly regretted it. That was where I had been when I announced that I wouldn't be coming home and when they guilted me into returning.

My father nodded and poured himself some more brandy, but he didn't refill my glass.

"You'd better sober up, Nicky," my father said. "Take a good, hard look at yourself."

I stared at my shoes, marveling at his ability to make me feel like I was ten years old again. Even when Daisy called me by that diminutive, it didn't carry the same condescension.

"I don't blame anyone," he continued with a heavy sigh. "You were going to turn out the way you are, no matter what. What I'm talking about is this restlessness of yours, this flitting about from here to there. I thought military service would solve it. Now, I worry about your lack of commitment more than I worry about your *questionable* proclivities. Are we clear?"

"Yes, Dad," I said, downing the dregs of my glass. "We're clear. I understand."

My father nodded gravely. "Just to make sure that you do, I'm giving you ten thousand and writing you out of my will. If you can't find a respectable place to live and get a foothold with that kind of money, then I don't know what hope there is for you."

I sat in stunned silence. He'd only given me four thousand to fund my New York venture, although he'd been under the impression that it would only last for a few months. This was sobering in comparison, as it wasn't one man's exile fee. It was enough for two.

"Dad, I don't—" I began, finding it difficult not to reveal that what I felt was more elation than devastation. "That is, I don't know what to say. That's very generous of you. And, yes, of course, I understand. It wouldn't be proper for you to . . . to . . . "

"Jay seems like a decent young man," my father said. "He grew up poor?"

"Very, very poor," I agreed. "So poor I can't even begin to imagine it, actually."

"Don't be selfish. If he ever wants to leave you, let him. Don't rob him of a life."

That was the point by which I'd had enough, no matter how generous his send-off.

"A life's what we hope we've got, Dad. Good night." I got up and left the study.

If Jay had any objections to my invading the guest room and climbing naked into bed beside him, he didn't give them. I'd become an expert at ridding him of pajamas even given the obstacle of bedclothes. I didn't care if it got back to my father by way of the housekeeper.

Perhaps absolute confirmation would prompt *him* to take a good, hard look.

Whether it was the ensuing week of only one spare bed actually seeing any use (and use it thoroughly, we did) or the fact that my father genuinely felt some kind of distant, abstract pity for Mr. Gatz, Jay and I were quietly shipped off to Edina. The hastily written check in my pocket was light as a feather but strangely comforting. The drive, which should have lasted about forty minutes, took well over an hour due to unexpectedly heavy snowfall.

Prudently, Jay had called ahead to inform his father of our arrival.

"I would of stayed inside if I knew you were running late," said the old man with watery eyes and an impressive gray beard who greeted us from the front porch. He'd clearly been waiting a while; he stood shivering in his cheap ulster. "I *would* of. Let me take those."

"We'll manage," Jay insisted, taking two of our bags. I followed him up the slippery front walk with the other two while snowflakes swirled, glittering cold around us. Once we'd got inside and shed our wet coats, Henry Gatz offered me one shaky hand.

"It's a real pleasure to make your acquaintance, Mr.—"

"Carraway," I said, shaking it. "I'm Nick Carraway."

"Jimmy tells me you met in the war," Mr. Gatz continued.

"Yes," I replied, catching Jay's wary expression. "We did."

In that modest yet comfortable house, there was only one spare bedroom. Mr. Gatz showed us to the door and then said he'd be in the kitchen when we were ready to eat. Until then, I'd failed to register the obvious aroma of roast chicken and potatoes.

"Well, this one's easy, old sport," Jay said, lightly kicking the spare mattress and set of linens his father had dug up somewhere and set on the floor beside the bed.

"I'll feel bad about not using that," I said. "He went to so much trouble."

"We can," Jay said, flipping the light switch on our way out. "If it'll set you at ease." I kissed him in the darkened hall, unhurried, while we listened to his father rattle around mumbling to himself with plates, silverware, and beer bottles in the kitchen.

Playing the veteran observer for the next handful of days while father and son caught up over cups of coffee and ragged family memorabilia was no hardship. Mr. Gatz had a fastidious little black house cat to keep him company, and she had instantly taken a liking to me for no reason other than that I'd scratched behind her ears when we first walked in.

"You be good now, Sassy," Mr. Gatz told her. She stretched in my lap and yawned.

"Where'd she get that name?" I asked, finding her rather too genteel for the moniker.

"She's called Sassafras," Jay volunteered. "After one of our dearly departed barn cats."

I scratched under her chin. She purred fit to rival Jay's infamous yellow Kissel's engine.

Whether it had been present in Jay from the start of our visit, I couldn't say, but by the time we'd been under his father's roof for a full week, I perceived that a restless melancholy had come to color

Jay's every gesture. He only seemed like himself when we were alone after hours, wrapped up together in the guest bed against the ferociously pervasive chill.

"Out with it," I said to him, finally. "If you're unhappy here, then we ought to leave."

"There's nothing I'd like more, Nick," Jay sighed, "but I feel obliged, you see. He was the only other person who gave a damn when I was shot, aside from you."

"It's his job to give a damn," I said, keeping half an eye on Sassy, who'd followed us into the room several hours earlier and was now crouched next to the door, occasionally pawing at it with a pitiful trill. "Estranged or not, he's your father. That counts."

"Was it your job to give a damn, too?" Jay asked. "My kindnesses to you could have been construed as bribery. Did you feel you had a say in the matter?"

Partly stung by the question and partly fed up with the cat's fuss, I picked my way out of bed, retrieved my underwear from the floor, and put them on before opening the door just a sliver. Sassy bolted without so much as rubbing up against my legs in thanks.

I closed the door and said, "Three months later, that's all you can think to ask?"

Jay's features crumpled as he sat up, badly skewing the covers, and reached for me.

"I didn't mean it like that," he insisted. "You have to understand; it's just that sometimes I have so much *doubt* about everything . . . "

Jay paused, and for a moment, I could hear his fretful voice on the other end of the line all those times he'd called me during the summer. I knew with fateful certainty that, if I'd been able to see his face during those conversations, *this* is what I would have seen.

"I shouldn't feel like that. Not with you. Nick, I—"

"You couldn't say it on the phone *or* to my face," I said, picking my way over the clothing-strewn spare mattress on the floor, "but you almost did. A handful of times, even. I heard it in your voice. I can hear it now. Is it that difficult?"

"I *do* need you," he said, patting the pillow. "Now, come keep me warm, old sport."

I went to him willingly, wondering why I'd even bothered getting partially dressed.

"I'll talk to your father tomorrow," I murmured later, what with both of us sated and more than half asleep. "People open up for me. Sometimes, they even listen."

Drowsily, Jay nodded, burrowing even closer against my shoulder.

Guiltily, I held him. Pettiness was something I'd need to unlearn.

I rose an hour earlier than usual the next morning, faced instantly with the challenge of disentangling myself from Jay without waking him. He slept deeply, although he was easy to rouse provided there was light in the room. As I had expected, Mr. Gatz was already seated in the kitchen with a plate of toast, the morning paper, and Sassy perched in his lap.

"Not so easy to wake up these days, that son of mine. Didn't used to be."

"He's got a lot on his mind lately," I said, helping myself to some coffee.

"Jimmy always did," said Mr. Gatz, and the pride in his voice was unmistakable. "Even as a kid, he was always thinking of ways he might better himself. Let me show you." He disappeared for a moment and returned carrying what looked like a ragged paperback. He put the book in my hands and resumed his seat, implying by gesture that I should open it.

"*Hopalong Cassidy*?" I asked. "What specific part am I looking for?"

"Inside the back cover," he said. "Go on, take a look. It just shows you."

Jay's childhood *Schedule*, dated 12 September 1906, was indeed thorough to a fault. He'd drifted a long way from rising at six o'clock in the morning, although he'd certainly succeeded where gaining poise and elocution was concerned. I had to smile at his resolve to stop smoking—endearingly ironic, especially now—and grant that he had finally made good on his promise to be better to his parents, or at least what was left of them.

"Jimmy was always making resolutions," said Mr. Gatz, rubbing his watery eyes. "For improving his mind, you see. For getting ahead in life, too. He was a great one for that. Sure enough, he's gone and done it. I had my doubts, but I should of known he would."

"Yes, he has," I agreed. "His latest venture's in Boston, so that's where we're headed."

"Great town, Boston, they say," Mr. Gatz mused. "Paul Revere's midnight ride, tea party in the harbor. I ain't never been there. Are you his business partner now, Mr.—"

"Carraway," I reminded him, too sleepy to feel irritated. "I guess I am."

"You've seen that grand house of his in New York, haven't you?" asked Mr. Gatz, taking out his wallet. He removed a worn photograph and handed it to me. My chest tightened at the sight. That fantastical, opulent monument to success was all gone now, all Wolfsheim's.

I nodded and handed the photograph back to Mr. Gatz, knowing what I had to do.

"He sold it. That's one of the decisions he made after he recovered," I said, hoping to God I'd learned a thing or two from Jay about lying. "The house would've been too big to maintain all the way from Boston, too much fuss to look after. We're turning the profits over on a place in Beacon Hill, putting the rest toward business costs. It's generous of him."

"You young'uns sure got the right idea," said Mr. Gatz, tapping his forehead. "Join up, double your fortunes, live frugally till you find the right gals to settle down with."

"That's why we've been so grateful for your hospitality, Mr. Gatz," I continued, and a creak from the hallway, too soft for the old man's ears to catch, alerted me to the likelihood of Jay's lurking presence. "As much as we'd like to stay longer, we'd better leave soon. This has been a wonderful respite before we get back to work."

"Good morning," Jay said, choosing that moment to make a spectacular show of yawning and stretching as he came into the kitchen. "I see you two have got a fine head start on setting the world to rights." He paused to scratch Sassy behind the ears.

"I won't keep you longer if you've got to go," said Mr. Gatz, tugging his beard in excitement. "You've got plans. Send me a picture of the new place."

"I will, Dad," Jay said and gave his father that dazzling smile. "I promise I will."

Our return journey to the East Coast passed in much the same fashion as our outward journey to the Middle West had done, with the notable exception that I made an effort to drink less, and Jay didn't smoke at all. As a result, the card games were less interesting, but the conversation, filled to the brim with flirtation, remained a thrill. And so, lacking much else to do, the blinds of our sleeper car stayed decisively drawn.

When I say that we found a modestly appointed townhouse in the outskirts of Beacon Hill, I mean that we spent at least two and a half weeks back at the Parker House before, between our individual widespread scouting efforts, we found a place that had been on the market for months. The wallpaper was peeling, and it was in sore need of flooring repairs.

Jay took one look at the small, shattered greenhouse in the brick-walled back garden, turned to me, and said, "Look, old sport. Your new writing studio."

"Tricky to heat," I said. "Can I write indoors during winter?"

"Depends," Jay replied, cracking half a smile. "If you do it by hand, sure, that's quiet enough. But if you bring home a typewriter, all bets are off."

"Fair," I said, grinning. "It'll be a change after living alone."

After the viewing, back in our suite, I confessed to Jay that even a price tag of five thousand—a bargain, given the view and the neighborhood—gave me pause. I confessed it was because I didn't know the first thing about making improvements and seriously doubted whether we could afford to bring in an appropriately skilled renovation team.

"That's where I come in," Jay said. "I've done it before, and I can do it again."

Suddenly, I'd never been more grateful for those rough years he'd spent taking work as and where he found it. From clam-digging to construction, no job was too daunting. If anything, I felt too useless to deserve what benefits I would gain from Jay's hard labor.

"You can't do it overnight, though," I insisted. "I don't think your doctors in New York would advise it. Furthermore, I won't *let* you. Is it habitable as it is? I mean, what if you were to pick at it slowly? You could show me a thing or two along the way so I can help."

Jay spent a moment or two turning this over in his mind before responding.

"Some of the ceiling plaster is cracked, but I didn't see any signs of water damage higher up than the ground floor walls," he said at length. "It's not comfortable, but it's livable."

"How long do you think it would take us to get it up to snuff?" I asked.

"As we are?" he replied with a grimace. "Six, seven months. Even a year."

"Just say the word," I told him. "If you're up for that, I'll make an offer."

Jay rolled me over onto the papers on which I'd been scribbling estimates, which was more than enough of an answer. I called the real estate agent first thing in the morning.

Of course, that anecdote brings us back to the present. Three years on, our house is presentable—if not elegant, by most people's standards. The greenhouse has even been sufficiently repaired, that I should be sitting here shivering in it, my coffee frigid.

Now, I occupy a middling editorial post at the *Boston Globe*, my dues in the bonds business having been paid. I pen a weekly gossip column that has garnered accolades on the grounds of containing cutting yet cleverly uplifting social satire. That's how one of my co-workers put it. I feel guilty for not knowing his name yet, despite repeatedly being told.

Normally, in these colder months, I would indeed have found myself writing indoors, watching Jay strip rotting wallpaper whilst in various fetching stages of undress. No job worth seeing through to loving completion is ever truly finished. Although the matter of the walls is well behind us, Jay has moved on to projects ever more refined in focus, right down to rearranging the mosaic tiles in the short hallway leading to the rickety cellar stairs.

And if the pattern he's chosen should happen to resemble one we both recall from a half-remembered dream—as viewed through sun-shot, bloody ripples of clear and finite blue—it doesn't bear mentioning again. By this time tomorrow, I'll be forgiven.

CHAPTER 4

The Busy and the Tired

O ne fine March morning in 1932—about a month after federal agents raided the speakeasy at 153 Causeway Street, on the only night Jay and I had ever been in it—I received a letter from the one person I had assumed least likely ever to seek contact with me again.

"Stay home," Jay murmured drowsily, draping one leg over my hip. "Can't the office make do without you today? You said last night that those columns write themselves."

"I told Taylor I'd be in an hour late today, just in case of *this*," I replied, trying to catch my breath where I'd lost track of it in the damp, familiar curve of Jay's neck. "At this rate, I'll be an hour and a half late. You're bad news for my career, Jay. You always have been."

"Then call in sick, old sport. I'll personally see to it you get plenty of bed rest."

"I love you," I told him, rising, and then bent back down for a swift parting kiss, "but I don't believe for a second that you'd let us pass the day restfully."

Jay studied me with an expression of the same distant, dreaming disbelief he'd shown the first time I said it—never mind that we'd *both* been saying it for the better part of what will amount to exactly a decade come September. I smiled to reassure him.

"And to think I'd been pining after the wrong cousin for so long," Jay said softly.

"You stopped in time," I teased him on my way out the door. "Jay, I've got to go."

THE PURSUED AND THE PURSUING

The postman stopped me on the front stairs. His brief, critical glare made me wonder if, in my haste to dress, I'd added an especially offensive ensemble to the already standing affront of lacking an attractive wife with whom he might flirt. The fault was with him, I reasoned, if he couldn't appreciate the sight of Jay in a tasteful dressing gown.

"Here's a letter, Mr. Carraway," he muttered and then stalked off down Pinckney Street.

"Good morning to you, too, Frank," I said, about to step onto the sidewalk, but just then, my eyes fell on the name written above the return address. My heart stopped.

I stood there, blinking for several minutes, but the offending letters didn't alter or rearrange themselves in the slightest. Behind me, the front door swung open. I felt violently ill. Jay slid an arm around my waist, and we sank down together on the bottom stair.

"Nick, what is it?" he asked, setting a hand on the letter, which I had turned over.

"The wrong cousin," I said, surrendering the envelope. "She's a goddamn *fool*."

"What we're going to do," Jay said, guiding me carefully to my feet, "is go back inside. You're going to sit down and have a drink of something that's not bourbon while I ring Taylor and explain that dinner last night simply didn't agree with you. Are we clear?"

"Are we going to open this while we're at it? I'd just as soon start up the fireplace."

"She's your family," said Jay, resigned, holding open the door. "It'd be rude not to."

I waited to open the ominous missive until Jay got back from the kitchen with a fully stocked tea tray. Jay sat down beside me on the sofa while our Mélange Hédiard steeped, draping one arm behind me and across the back cushion with a casual yet fiercely possessive air.

I unfolded the letter with trembling fingers, and we both started to read.

Dearest Nick,

How appalling my manners are—nine years! It was such dreadful business, wasn't it, a very bad time, there's no denying that, and we must hope it's all turned out for the best. Still, I must be brave and write to you. Tom and I spent Christmas in Chicago, and who did we meet up with but dear old Aunt Meredith? She asked me if I knew how you were getting on in Beantown. I told her I had no idea that's where you were. I thought you'd stayed in New York. She says you've been living with a nice young man you met in the war, which is an awful shame, Nicky. Jordan's been married to some Asheville caddie for almost six years now—can you imagine? It could have been you. Pammy turns thirteen in April. It's for her sake I got your address from Aunt Meredith. Pammy's grown ever so fond of history, and Auntie reckons there's no place so full of history as Boston, or Philadelphia, or Washington. Well, look, we'd like to come visit you—that is, I mean Pammy and me. I'm afraid Tom wants nothing to do with you anymore. I've tried to make him understand, but those rumors about you that went around at Yale are gospel now as far as he's concerned (we've got to beat your sort down right along with the other races . . .). Nicky, I don't care if the rumors are true—that's not the part that scares me. But I'm afraid of what else I've heard, so very afraid, and Pammy's positively begging to see Boston now she knows you're there. Tom says I ought to take her just to give him some peace and quiet. I just don't know what to do. I should have called you, but Aunt Meredith didn't give me your telephone number, and I didn't want to ask. Nicky, I'll give you mine—please call. I'm so sorry for so very many things, and if what else Aunt Meredith said is true, I just can't bear to think—!

Your DAISY

Her phone number was scrawled across the bottom, a quavering postscript.

"Matches," I muttered, struggling to my feet, almost knocking the tea tray off the coffee table. "This is a disaster, Jay. No way in hell am I letting her smash up our life."

Jay stood behind me at the sink and watched three-quarters of the letter burn before turning on the faucet and shaking the charred remnant—her phone number—dry.

"She owes you an apology," he said. "She's making it the only way she knows how."

"She owes *you* a fucking apology," I snarled, shocked into silence by my own venom.

Jay rested his cheek against the back of my head, his hands on my shoulders, breathing hard. I held the wet fragment in my open, ash-smudged palms, my vision blurring. I wanted to fill the sink, plunge it underwater, and hold it there until the paper disintegrated like snow.

"Never forget," Jay whispered. "It's you I chose in the end, *you* I'm holding."

"That's the part that scares *me* most," I said. "What she might do on account."

I stood there choking on the sentiment while Jay made his way purposefully over to the telephone, dialed the *Globe*, and told Taylor not to expect me until Wednesday. I dropped Daisy's number and dashed over, taking hold of his arm, but he'd hung up by then.

Jay was stronger than I was. He half dragged, half carried me back upstairs to bed.

"What's the worst thing that could happen?" he asked once he'd got me tucked in.

"Make us both completely miserable by talking nonstop about Tom and Jordan."

"I don't think she's likely to do that. She'd have Pammy with her, remember?"

"She barely believes her own child is real, so why do you think that'd stop her?"

Jay sighed and sat down on the edge of the bed. He had an infuriatingly soothing way of leading me through the logical fallacies induced by fits of panic. I wasn't as calm as I'd been a decade ago, and, conversely, Jay wasn't as excitable. We'd come full circle.

"We wouldn't need to stop her, Nick," he said firmly, taking my hand against the coverlet, "because she wouldn't dare try. Do you know why that is?"

I shook my head, even though I could guess. I wanted to hear him say it.

"I won't let her," Jay said, squeezing my hand. "That's all there is to it."

"You got your way," I mumbled late the next morning around a mouthful of toast. "You always do. Here I am. Traumatized, debauched, and out two days' wages."

"More debauched than traumatized," Jay said, adjusting the pillows behind us. "I've got a consultation on Thursday and a repair job on Saturday. Don't worry, old sport."

"You've got till eight tomorrow morning. What *else* are you going to do with me?"

"Talk some sense into you now that you're sufficiently bedded and fed," he said. "You've overworked yourself again. You wouldn't have reacted to the letter like that if you hadn't spent all last weekend chained to the typewriter and drinking—"

"The columns write themselves, yes," I pointed out, "but the novel sure doesn't."

"It won't if you force it," said Jay and put what was left of the toast in my hand.

"What's this about talking sense into me?" I asked, forcing myself to eat the rest.

"I do think," replied Jay, calmly, "that you should give Daisy a call this evening."

"And I think you're crazy," I said, tossing our empty plate on the floor, in the mood to fight now that I didn't feel faint. The plate didn't shatter, as it had landed on the rug, but the impact made Jay flinch.

"We've been free of them all for years, Jay. I know you have noble intentions, but *why* would you think that's even a *remotely* sound idea?"

Jay stared at his hands folded in his lap and then fetched my tea off the nightstand.

"Closure," he said, pressing the mug between my palms. "It did *me* a world of good."

I raised the mug to my lips and cursed into the lukewarm, over-steeped dregs.

"If I let her speak her piece, will you let it go? I hate them, maybe her most of all."

"This isn't about me letting go. I did that a long time ago, Nick. This is about you."

I shook my head and handed the empty, sticky mug back to him, utterly disgusted.

"Daisy very nearly got you killed—*twice*, might I add—and didn't even care to come see you in the hospital, much less send a card. They're careless people, Jay. Remember? Careless, hateful, *danger-ous* people. You're still worth more to me than the whole damn lot."

"Are we any less so," he asked quietly, "you and I? After our part, what *we've* done?"

"Jordan's a real survivor," I said, despising how easily she'd put it all behind her.

"And so are we," Jay insisted. He tugged the covers up over us and rolled me onto my back. "Daisy's not going to steal me away if that's what you're afraid of. She's thinking of her daughter as a real person, which is more than she ever did before."

I recalled the solemn, self-possessed blonde toddler we'd each once greeted in turn. She'd had quick, restless eyes like her father and unusual articulacy for a child of three.

"Thirteen," I said pensively. "With an avid interest in history, no less. There go her mother's hopes for her, dashed to pieces." I swal-lowed my impulse toward laughter, abruptly serious. "Where'd the time go, anyway? What happened to the future we imagined?"

Jay gave an indignant huff and kissed me soundly, at least in part to shut me up.

"Back then, what I imagined was a farce. And you didn't imagine anything."

"Because I wasn't brave enough," I said. "I've told you before. I'm a coward."

"Then you have no choice but to face her," Jay implored. "Prove yourself wrong."

"You have so much faith in me," I marveled, shifting slowly under him. "Why?"

Even as Jay's eyes closed, his lips parted. "You kept—Nick, I *stayed* for you."

That was how, several hours later, I ended up disheveled in Jay's dressing gown on the sofa with the telephone cradle in my lap and the receiver clutched to my ear in sheer terror. Jay sat down beside me, indulging in a rare cigarette. He held it out every now and again so that I could take a slow drag in order to steady my jangling nerves.

"Things went from bad to worse." I sighed and, in a puff of smoke, finally dialed.

Jay's arm slipped from the back of the sofa, settling across my shoulders while it rang.

The butler, whose curt tone I knew instantly, answered. "Buchanan residence—"

"No, Henri, let *me*," said a young, unfamiliar voice, female but unquestionably inflected with a touch of Tom's haughty forthrightness. "Mother said I should practice." The girl cleared her throat. "Hello, this is the Buchanan residence. May I ask who is speaking?"

"This—" I hesitated, fixing Jay with a panicked expression, "—this is Nick Carraway. Pammy, is that you? Why, hello there. I haven't seen you since you were *three*."

"It's Pam now," she said crossly, "but Mother will never learn. Are you Uncle Nicky?"

"Well, I'm—" Jay held the cigarette to my lips and made an

encouraging gesture, "—yes, I suppose I am. You can call me whatever you like. Is your mother at home?"

"She says I'm to speak to you for her," said Pam. "It'll be good experience if I arrange the visit. I'll call you Uncle Nick because Nicky's no better than Pammy, is it? Oh, *Mother*, stop making faces. Mother *is* here. I think this isn't just for practice but because she's afraid. You must be awfully smart, Uncle Nick, to make Mother so afraid," the girl continued, and I felt a thrill of hope at the winking sarcasm in her voice. "Mother's *very* afraid of smart people."

At this juncture, I heard a struggle in which the phone got wrestled away from Pam.

"As you might have guessed," said Daisy, breathlessly, "I can't take her anywhere."

"Oh, I don't know about that," I said coolly. "I think Boston will like her just fine."

"Listen, Nicky," she said. "You've changed. You've changed, and I don't like it one bit."

"It sounds to me like you haven't changed at all. Charming Daisy Fay. We'll be glad to have the two of you come visit, of course. We've got a nice brownstone in Beacon Hill."

Jay held my hand, tolerating how I squeezed his fingers tighter with every word.

"We'll be delighted," she snapped. "Aunt Edith said you live with some man."

"That's right," I replied, keeping my voice even. "You'll get on like old friends."

"Delightful," said Daisy, resigned. "When shall we plan to visit you, Nicky?"

I heard Pam in the background, catching the words *Mother, don't call him—*

"My schedule at the paper is negotiable," I said, because, inasmuch as I complained to Jay about his occasional machinations to keep me home for a day or two, it was true.

"What about next month?" Daisy asked, feigning nonchalance.

"We'll come up on the first and stay for a week. I despise traveling by train, but there's nothing for it."

"Where are you?" I asked, suddenly aware I'd blanked her letter's return address.

"Alexandria. Tom likes being close to Washington. He's grown very political."

Jay must have overheard what she'd said because his expression turned sour.

"Washington must like having him," I said, stroking the back of Jay's hand.

"You must think you're very funny. Does that man you live with think so?"

"What, you mean Jay?" I asked. "He thinks I'm a riot. See you on the first."

I hung up on her, trembling hard enough to rattle the receiver in its cradle.

"I don't care whether it's wise or not," I said, "but I *really* need a drink."

Jay kissed me and got up, crossing the room to where we kept the decanters.

"I'm not about to argue with that," he replied, returning with two glasses.

We sipped bourbon in silence for a while, each of us lost in his own thoughts. In one respect, Jay had been right. One conversation with Daisy, and I already felt emboldened. I had stood my ground. Gradually, it was the exchange with Pam to which my thoughts circled back.

"Pam's more precocious than ever," I observed. "I hope you won't mind a teenager."

"I was a teenager once myself," Jay said sardonically. "I can manage to host one."

"You won't be doing it alone," I reminded him, lighting another cigarette. "You won't let Daisy get to me, and I won't let Pam get to you. That's a reasonable division of labor."

Jay nodded, looking like he wanted to smile, but couldn't bring himself to do it.

"I understand why you have reservations. I was putting on a brave face yesterday."

"Well, your brave face did the trick. If you don't let me back down, I won't let you."

***

"The house isn't ready," I lamented, surveying our morning's hand-iwork. "It'll never be ready. I feel less anxious about our New Year's parties. How can that be?"

"Leave the house as it is," Jay said, steering me over to the sofa.

I grudgingly sat down, careful not to wrinkle my jacket, and regarded Jay suspiciously when he knelt down in front of me on the floor, heedless of his pristine trousers.

"We might even live in it a little," he suggested, reaching for my belt, "to compensate for the tidying. I can't answer your question about the parties. I feel fine about those."

I caught his fingers halfway through unfastening the buckle and demanded, breathing too shallowly, "What are you *doing*? They'll be here in forty-five minutes."

"Living a little. Distracting you from imaginary chores," Jay coaxed. "I couldn't possibly stop now, you see, not with you in such a state. I've got to do something about it."

"Be . . . *God*, Jay, be quick about it," I hissed, giving in because his clever, inevitable mouth was already in the one place I most urgently needed it.

Twenty minutes later, the doorbell rang. Jay swore when I stopped what I was doing, and we both toppled indignantly off the sofa. There was a frantic rush to set our clothes to rights.

"Make it up to me later," Jay said, tugging me to my feet. "Always worth the wait."

"Let's hope the walls aren't too thin," I muttered. The doorbell rang a second time.

"I'm afraid they are," Jay replied. He was staring apprehensively at the doorknob.

"Forget the house," I said, taking the steps required to turn it. "Just like you said."

Pam stood motionless on the front stoop, ahead of her mother, blotting Daisy out.

"Uncle Nick?" she ventured, breaking into a smile that made me forget everything.

Pam was almost as tall as her father, no mean feat for her age. In response to my mute, astonished nod, she dropped her clutch on the welcome mat and threw her arms around me. I swayed back into the house, bearing my lively, affectionate burden across the threshold without stumbling into Jay. She had so much warmth in her slender frame.

"That's no way to greet a stranger, precious," Daisy said, pulling the door shut as she stepped inside. She narrowed her dark eyes, tapping Pam impatiently on the shoulder.

The girl hadn't let go of me, and she seemed to have no intention of doing so.

"Do you remember him so well?" Daisy went on. "You were only a baby."

"I remember his face," Pam said against my shoulder. "It's such a kind face."

I set one hand between Pam's shoulder blades, nodding to Daisy in greeting.

Jay stepped up beside me and bent to study Pam with his warmest smile. I wondered if she'd see in that smile what I'd first seen in it—if it's what she remembered about him.

"My name is Pamela Buchanan," said the girl, letting go of me in favor of shyly offering Jay her hand. "You must be Uncle Nick's mysterious gentleman friend."

"My name is James Gatz," he told Pam, giving her gloved knuckle a polite, pantomimed peck. "You can call me Jay. All of my closest friends do. Your mother always did."

"Mother didn't say she knew you, too," said Pam, tilting her blond, bobbed head.

Jay let go of Pam's hand and turned to Daisy—as if she were a mere incidental, an afterthought. I felt breath returning to my lungs in great, relieved gasps. I didn't realize I'd grown dizzy or lost my footing until Jay had me by one arm and Pam had me by the other.

They planted me firmly in the nearest armchair. Daisy just stared, wringing her hands.

"Mother, go get him some water!" Pam pleaded, already on her knees beside me. "I can see the kitchen right through there. Look what a shock you've given your poor, dear cousin! Is this how you treat everybody you haven't seen in years and years?"

"Mrs. Buchanan, please have a seat," Jay said, indicating the sofa. "I'll see to it."

While Jay clattered around the kitchen, Daisy sat watching me with a mix of unabashed resentment and intense concern. She watched Pam fuss over me with curious detachment, too flummoxed to scold the girl for dabbing at my cheeks with her pristine, wadded-up white gloves and checking my forehead for an elevated temperature with her bare hands.

"You haven't been following the doctor's orders, have you, Nicky?" Daisy asked.

"I'm not seeing any doctor," I told her. "There's nothing wrong with me at all."

"He hasn't got a fever, Mother," said Pam, getting to her feet. "He's just flustered."

"No," said Daisy, "but it doesn't take an expert to see he's drinking too much."

Pam went over and sat on the sofa, claiming the opposite end from her mother.

"It's a dangerous proposition," said Daisy, glancing from me to Jay in the kitchen and then back to me, "taking up with a man when you don't know what he's really worth."

"I know exactly what we're worth," I told her. "I write for a living. He fixes boats."

"A writer!" Pam exclaimed. "That's so *exciting.* And Jay—does he really fix boats?"

"Only the finest in Boston Harbor," Jay said, bearing in a tray laden with a pitcher of water and the half-carafe of leftover lemonade from the day before. "I'll take you out to see the one I'm working on in a few days if you like. The owner would love to have you."

"Nicky used to court Aunt Jordan," Daisy said as Jay filled glasses. "Remember?"

"No," said Pam. "I just remember you sitting together around that great big table."

"She was useful," I told Daisy. "We all found each other useful back then, right?"

"Daddy says Aunt Jordan's a freeloader," Pam said. "See, Mother? We're useful."

I'm not sure how Jay kept a straight face as he parceled out glasses. First, there was water for me. Next, lemonade for Pam. There was water for Daisy and then water for himself.

Helplessly, I started to laugh, and Pam, who'd been smirking as it was, joined in.

"I don't know what I'll do," Daisy said. "I can't be seen in public with any of you."

"Jay's very polite, Mother," said Pam. "The two of you can walk a few steps behind."

"I'm afraid not," Jay said, claiming the chair next to mine. "I'm already spoken for."

When Daisy looked at me again, it wasn't with reproach. Her eyes radiated *relief.*

"Pammy spent the whole trip inventing itineraries. Why don't you share, precious?"

Pam made an irked face and sipped her lemonade. "We only just got here, *Mother*."

"We can make it up as we go along," Jay said. "There's no rush. No rush at all."

"A fine claim coming from *you*," Daisy replied. "Mr. Plan Everything to a Fault."

"We've learned to live a little," I said, unwilling to risk things getting out of hand.

Just then, Pam threw her wadded-up gloves at Daisy with impressive accuracy.

"Don't be a bully," she said to her mother and then glanced apologetically at Jay. "I'm sorry about that. It can't be helped sometimes. She learned it from Daddy."

Jay and I exchanged looks of deepest, most profound relief. With Pam around to battle Daisy, what need did we have of each other as knights in shining armor?

Like Jay, Pam was an early riser. I came downstairs on the first official morning of their visit to find the two of them seated at the table with plates of crisp bacon and runny eggs.

"Uncle Nick, we saved some for you," Pam said, pointing to a covered plate on the counter. "Don't worry about Mother. She'll sleep as long as you let her."

"Then we should let her," I said, fetching the plate and joining them at the table.

"Pam was telling me all of the supposedly interesting things she's read about Boston," Jay explained, winking as he pointed at her with his fork. "Some of it was even true."

"Jay doesn't think Boston is interesting," Pam said. "Do *you* think it's interesting?"

"Interesting enough to live here," I replied. "If Jay doesn't think so, he can move."

"I see how it is," Jay said sadly. "You'll bookworm me out of house and home."

"You can't bookworm someone out of something," Pam protested. "It's not a verb."

"Take that back," I said, giving Pam a mock reproachful look. "It is so. And Jay should know because I've bookwormed him out of plenty."

Choosing that moment to take up comedy wasn't the wisest choice I'd ever made. Daisy had been watching us from the doorway, faintly scandalized, for God knew how long.

"Don't fill her head full of nonsense," Daisy said, sliding into the chair beside me.

Pam made an exaggerated show of shoving the last of her bacon into her mouth.

"I thought you wanted me to have a head full of nonsense," she said tauntingly.

I scooted my plate over to Daisy because I'd barely touched the food anyway. It felt like the only apology I could reasonably offer for Jay and I getting on so well with Pam.

"Eat your breakfast, Nicky," Daisy said, scooting it back. "I'm not hungry."

Jay wiped his mouth with one of the linen napkins he and Pam hadn't touched.

"I can make something else if you like. There's Bisquick in the cupboard. Newfangled, but all it's cracked up to be. We were impressed when it hit the shelves last year."

"How vulgar," Daisy said dryly. "Jay, don't trouble yourself on my account."

Pam shoved her own plate at Daisy. "Our hosts made breakfast, Mother."

Watching Daisy take implied orders from a thirteen-year-old was quite possibly the most satisfying thing I had ever seen. As Daisy cut resentfully into the single remaining egg on Pam's plate, Jay was blinking at the young woman in unabashed admiration.

"I thought we could go to Faneuil Hall today," Pam suggested.

"We can go anywhere you want," I said, heedless of my stolen heart.

In the days that followed, Daisy didn't waste any time in keeping out of Pam's way. She looked on while her daughter chattered gaily to Jay and me about anything and everything that crossed her mind. Pam knew exactly the effect her behavior was having, too—leading me to wonder if she was aware just how much she'd learned from her parents. Still, she was using those tactics in Jay's favor. I could tell she felt like Jay ran the risk of feeling left out, surrounded by three people related by blood. Daisy's watchful resentment felt like a badge of honor.

Where Faneuil Hall had been an excuse for Pam to rattle off all the facts she knew about the site, it had been little more than a glorified shopping trip for Daisy. She'd vanished for the several hours that Jay and I followed Pam around, locals being given a tour of our own city. I might have found Pam's stalwartness endearing if not for the fact that she hid her resentment of Daisy's neglect behind her perpetual thorny wit. I could tell that Jay perceived it, too.

That evening, I tried to work up the nerve to corner Daisy and confront her about it, but Daisy retired early, citing a headache. In her shoes, I supposed I'd have a headache, and that was when I realized she'd been dreading the visit just as much. I mentioned the epiphany to Jay after we'd said good night to Pam and sent her upstairs. He was satisfied to hear it but not smugly so.

We spent their second full day in town touring the Harvard campus. This was of genuine interest to me, as I'd never bothered to poke around my alma mater's chief rival. Jay enjoyed the experience on account of the architecture, and that was where Pam learned a few things from him. I was content to let the two of them talk. Before I knew it, Daisy and I had fallen behind.

"We need to talk, Nicky," she said when Pam and Jay were finally far enough ahead to be out of earshot. "This bad blood's not doing either of us any good."

"I don't know," I said, evading her attempt to take hold of my arm. "It's done me plenty."

"You think you've got the moral high ground because Pammy's thoroughly charmed."

"No, Daisy. I think I've got the moral high ground because I didn't hit a woman and run."

"You couldn't let it rest, could you?" Daisy whispered. "You've been dying to say that."

"You destroy people's lives," I said. "Don't destroy Pam's because she's inconvenient."

"That's harsh, Nicky," Daisy said tearfully. "Harsh and cold. You were always so kind. Even Pammy could see it when she was small. She thinks you still are."

"I'm not perfect," I said, realizing that barb had stung more than it should have, "but I'd like to think I have something resembling a moral compass."

Daisy shot me a withering glance, which never boded well for what she'd say next.

"How much of a compass could it be if it pointed you to take up with a fraud? He pulled the wool over my eyes, Nicky. For *years*. Don't let him pull it over yours."

I thought that over for about a minute, letting Daisy stew. It didn't hurt nearly as much as the insult involving Pam, who I'd come to care for inordinately in only a few days' time. I could only conclude it was because I was unwaveringly secure in what I felt for Jay.

"If I'm not kind, then I'm a fraud, too. Jay believes that I have integrity, but since you've pointed out that's not true . . . " I spread my hands. "We've pulled the wool over each other's."

There must have been something beyond the pale in that statement because Daisy began to laugh. Not her usual airy, girlish laughter, either. She had succumbed to jaded resignation.

"We all found each other useful," Daisy said at last, wiping her eyes. "We'll have to settle for an armistice, Nicky. There's nothing left for us otherwise."

"Your letter was a shock," I admitted. "You said you didn't know what to do. I didn't know what to do, either. I couldn't tell what your intentions were."

"I *had* no intentions when I wrote that letter," Daisy said, "except to get Pammy to quit nagging, and . . . " She sighed guiltily. "And to see if what Aunt Meredith said was true."

"You knew the man was Jay from the way she described him, didn't you?"

"I knew it was Jay because she said he was a war hero named James Gatz."

"I don't know what to tell you," I said, shrugging. "Is your curiosity satisfied?"

"You were always starry-eyed for him," Daisy said quietly, staring ahead to where Pam and Jay had paused to stare up at an inscrutable window. "The way I should have been."

"We joke about how he was chasing the wrong cousin," I said. "At least you can admit that the joke's true. I was afraid . . . Daisy, you *know* what I was afraid of."

"I don't want him back," Daisy said with curious gentleness. "I didn't want him back ten years ago, and I don't want him back now. I'm happy for you, Nicky."

After that, I held my tongue, wishing in vain that I could say the same for her.

Jay had a way with Pam that was a source of continual amazement. For all that he'd been nervous about sharing space with someone so young, he nonetheless had the impulse to turn his singular, magnanimous focus on her. Just when I thought our Harvard jaunt had been the pinnacle of that phenomenon, Jay exceeded it on our visit to the Museum of Fine Arts.

"There's so much to see," Pam said, staring at the directory of galleries, visibly overwhelmed. "I don't even know where to start, and we only have a few days left."

"Don't think about that," Jay said, setting a hand on her shoulder. "Sometimes, you've got to just exist in the moment. Do you ever get tired of looking ahead?"

"All the time," Pam said and then looked at me. "Do you, Uncle Nick?"

Given that Daisy had opted to stay home and recuperate from all the walking we'd been doing, I felt freer to speak my mind in Pam's presence. The relief was immense.

"I tried to do that when I was young. I rarely managed to see what was coming."

Pam was studying the directory again, thoughtful. "Mother says I'm a lot like you."

Jay gently squeezed her shoulder and then released it. "You're two peas in a pod."

"I like you both very much," Pam said. "Which gallery do you want to see first?"

"Egyptian," I said, when in fact, I would've been fine with anything given I had them both at my side. Daisy's absence had opened a chasm of emotion I was struggling to define.

"Good choice, old sport," Jay said, looking relieved that I had answered first, and then smiled at Pam. "Let's follow your Uncle Nick. He's clever and has fine taste."

Pam consulted the directory one last time, spinning on her heel to lead the way.

"You're the one with fine taste," she said. "You picked my uncle for a friend."

Pam's laconic diagnosis of our situation lacked only the romantic element. The elation Pam's perceptiveness incited in me was enough to let me forget Daisy entirely. We wandered one gallery after another—Egyptian, Greco-Roman, Early Americas. By then, it was time for lunch, so we backtracked to the museum café. Pam enthusiastically paid for everything.

"I'm starting to wonder," Jay said under his breath as we hung back to let Pam stare reverently at a Monet, "who's really spoiling whom. What about you?"

"I have *no* idea how she's turning out so well," I said, watching Pam step as close to the painting as she could without risking the gallery steward's intervention.

"Enjoy it while it lasts," Jay replied, subtly extending his fingers toward mine.

Nodding, I brushed the back of Jay's hand. I wanted to preserve that exquisite moment in amber—or, failing that, capture it in the only medium I knew how.

<hr />

"It's beautiful here," Pam murmured, perusing the graves at King's Chapel. "Look at their sad, ancient faces with sad, round eyes. What did you say they're called, Uncle Nick?"

"*Effigies*," I said, studying the nearest headstone. "*Memento mori.*"

"Dazzle us," said Daisy. "Translate. You went to Yale, after all."

Pam looked up, smiling conspiratorially. "Daddy went to Yale, too. Did you know?"

"I knew *him*," I said. "We were there at the same time, I mean.

Daisy met your father because of me, I'm rather ashamed to say. At a polo reception in New Haven."

"I didn't know *that*," Jay said, still regarding the stone, "but I might've guessed."

"How sordid we are," Daisy said, wrapping her fur coat tighter against the chill. "Sordid, entangled, and incestuous. There's so much you don't know, precious."

Pam shied from her mother's fawning hands, sidling ever closer to Jay and me.

"I don't want to know everything, Mother. Not everything about *you*, anyway. I'd rather know about these dead people and about who carved the sad faces. I'll write a report about them for school. *Memento mori*, Uncle Nick. What does that mean?"

"It's just basic Latin," I said. "I'm not brilliant. It means *remember that you will die.*"

"You're brilliant compared to Daddy," Pam said disdainfully, tucking her hair behind her ears. "He can't even translate basic French." She stepped even closer to Jay and me, whispering, "I don't know how he got into Yale. He's not very bright."

"If you lack smarts, money can get you in," Jay said. "It can get you lots of things."

"Daddy does have lots of money," Pam said, pensive as she stared at her expensive shoes against the brick walkway. "Mother said you were poor and that you used to live in a charming little shack across the bay from our old house. Even if it was little, I don't think you could have done that in New York if you were poor. You're not poor *now*. You live up on the same hill where all of the rich people in Boston live, in the same kind of house."

"I was lucky enough to go to Yale because *my* father has money," I admitted. "You might say I was also intelligent, and that helped. Or, well . . . maybe I only *thought* I was intelligent. I spent a lot of time making stupid decisions, letting my father pay for all of them."

"I don't want to do that," said Pam and then looked at Jay. "Did you go to college?"

"I started to," he said. "I went to Oxford, right after the war. But I didn't get to finish."

Pam's eyes went as round as the ones carved into the headstones. "Oxford in *England*?" she asked, disbelieving. "Did you go to London? Did you see Big Ben?"

"I did," Jay said and shot me a sidelong smile. "Your uncle and I went back to visit in the winter of twenty-two. We went to Canada first, and then on to England and France."

"What a splendid honeymoon," said Daisy, wryly. "I got stuck with Kapiolani."

"I think Europe sounds *much* more romantic than Hawaii," said Pam, and then paused for a moment before the next headstone, as if she'd only just realized she'd been complicit in a joke she could only partly understand. "But I know it wasn't one," she added, turning to Jay and me with apologetic haste. "A honeymoon, I mean."

"I don't know," said Jay, thoughtfully. "You could argue that honeymoons aren't just for people who can get married. People who enjoy each other's company go traveling together all the time. I believe it is, after a particular fashion, romantic."

By the end of that statement, Pam was smiling at him, more than a bit dazzled.

"We only have two days left," she murmured. "I wish we'd done everything."

Daisy made a pained sound and covered her mouth, striding toward the gate. Another thing we had in common was how easily words summoned emotional memories to the foreground—as if they'd happened yesterday. Whatever it was this time, I hadn't been party to it.

"We'll take the train from North Station out to Salem," I said. "How's that?"

"Hawthorne's house is there!" said Pam, hopefully. "I read *The Scarlet Letter*."

"The day before you leave, I'll take you out to see that yacht," Jay promised.

When we got back to the house, Daisy went straight upstairs and retired early. Pam had been less than thrilled about sharing the guest bedroom with her mother, I could tell, but she'd borne sharing the plush queen-size with considerable grace for her age.

While Pam sat reading Eliot's latest collected volume of verse, which I'd bought for her at the Grolier in Cambridge, I followed Jay into the kitchen and closed the door behind us.

"Do you know what she told me on the way back home, old sport?"

"More than you bargained for, I imagine. You've been very patient."

"She's heard about the women's colleges up here. She wants to go."

"Daisy will have a fit," I said, and then: "What about Wellesley?"

"Exactly," Jay agreed. "We'd never see her if she went to Smith."

We spent the next thirty seconds or so staring at each other, at first in dismay—and then, gradually, in startled, silent laughter. What had been intended as a visit of reconciliation had somehow led to us planning a future for the daughter of a woman we'd both tried our best to forget. I realized Daisy would become a fixture in our sphere again because, after the events of that week, I doubted either of us could imagine life without Pam.

I leaned into Jay's embrace, crushing my mouth against his shoulder until the fit of hilarity subsided. Once it did, Jay tilted my chin up and pressed his lips to mine.

"Oh," said a voice from the doorway, wondering yet unsurprised. "I see."

We drew apart quickly but didn't let go of each other. It seemed absurd.

"You're rather odd," Pam said. "I don't mind. Daddy does, but he thinks anybody who's different from him hardly counts as a person. I suppose you share that other room all the time, don't you, not just when somebody comes to visit from out of town. I'm sorry," she faltered. "I won't tell anyone. I like you too much. I *promise* I won't tell. I'm going to bed now."

Unthinking, I let go of Jay and went over to fold the terrified girl in my arms. Her brief, nervous monologue had risen and risen in pitch until she was choking on hysterics.

"It's all right," I said and felt her tears dampen my shirt. "You can stay up and read for as long as you want. Sleep on the sofa for all we care. This place is safe."

"I know," Pam hiccupped, clutching desperately at my arms. "I *know*."

Before retiring, we made her tea and saw to it she had a pillow and blankets.

"It's not right, what she has to put up with," I said bitterly, letting Jay strip me of my shirt. "She's young, but she's smarter than anybody I've met in a long time. I can't figure out how two people like Tom and Daisy produced—well, *her*."

"We can only watch and wait," said Jay, consolingly, already out of everything except his underwear. "We can also make sure she knows she has two sets of ears and a roof over her head should she need it, although in my estimation, we're not parenting material."

I sat down on the edge of the mattress, running my fingers through my hair.

"I didn't ask for this either, Jay. I just wanted to be rid of them, not to *care*."

"You need to stop worrying so much," Jay said, tugging on my wrist until I crawled up to join him against the pillows. He was naked by now, and my desire to match him state for state resulted in an awkward scramble. He pulled me close once I'd succeeded in the ridiculous endeavor, arranging us so that we lay side by side, facing each other. "So do I."

"That's all I've ever done," I said. "About everything. Don't know how to stop."

"At least stop fretting for right now," Jay chided. "That would be a fine start."

I kissed him until the sense of sleepiness I'd been fighting off transformed into something else entirely. My body remembered the interruption of five days ago, of the kitchen some fifteen minutes before, and decided wholeheartedly that it would not tolerate another.

When the floorboards creaked just outside our door in the hall, I froze and swore. For a moment, I could feel nothing but the chaotic, startled clamor of our hearts.

Someone was hovering in the hallway or had been there mere moments ago.

"Do you remember that first afternoon, after I got home from the hospital?" Jay asked, trailing one finger from my shoulder down the back of my arm. He was moving again, moving me right along with him, and I couldn't have resisted even if I'd tried.

"If I ever forget, it'll mean my mind's gone and—*Christ*, Jay. It's no use."

"You felt so good," he murmured, "feel so good right *now*, you drive me—"

I couldn't respond, except with a groan. I'd already tensed, trembling against him, spending far too soon. If Daisy really was listening at the door, I didn't spare her. Jay didn't spare her, either. I held him fast, through who he'd both been and become, and my name gasped raggedly over and over was the only enchantment I'd ever need.

"If Pam enjoyed King's Chapel today, she'd go nuts for Old Burying Point in Salem," I said drowsily, after cleaning us up and killing the lights. "The girl loves ghosts."

"She's learned to live with them early," Jay said. "I believe that'll serve her well."

If Pam's arrival meant our world was changing, then we'd live to change with it.

***

The day before Pam and Daisy were set to leave came sooner than we would've liked.

"Do you see that outcrop, right there on the edge of the shore?" Jay asked, raising his voice over the wind's roar. "That's called Egg

Rock. Looks like the footpath is flooded out today. That's not always an island. Next time, we'll approach by land and hike to it."

"Egg Rock," Daisy muttered into her furs. "Now you're just being cruel."

"No, that's what it's called," I reassured her, giving Pam a wink. "There's an inscription on it dating to 1885. It documents some tragic local history."

Pam stepped up beside Jay at the prow, squinting into the fierce blue sky.

"It's 1932," she said, "so that's . . . almost fifty years ago."

"Wrong Egg Rock, old sport," Jay clarified. "This one's also called Elephant Rock. The one with the inscription is landlocked in Concord. Relates to European theft of Nipmuc land."

"I read about that," Pam said sullenly, shading her eyes. "We're the barbaric ones."

If Tom could hear her, he'd have a fit. The thought warmed my chilled bones.

"Thoreau and Emerson used to sit out there," I said. "Have you read them?"

"Wrong rock," Jay repeated, approaching smug since I'd slipped again.

"I don't think," Pam admitted. "I know who they are, though. Whitman, too."

"Your uncle's a great fan of Whitman," Jay told her. "Wilde, Shakespeare . . . "

"I've read a few of Shakespeare's plays," Pam said. "I like the funny ones best."

"That's where you and your uncle will have to agree to disagree," Daisy said.

I pointed to our port of call looming in the near distance. "Lynn, Lynn, the City of Sin—you never come out the way you went in!" I chanted. "Come on. Say it with me, Pam."

"Nicky, how vulgar," Daisy murmured, but she recited it along with the rest of us.

We'd been blessed with bright, stiff wind for our passage. Pam had shrieked gleefully that morning when Jay told her I hadn't meant what I said about us taking the train to Salem. He then announced he'd sail us to Lynn on the yacht he'd mentioned—which was, in fact, ours.

I hadn't had the heart to reproach him for his joke regarding the owner some days before; Pam's delight at the surprise had far outweighed Jay's sly deception. She seemed disappointed that we'd need to book a car from Lynn to Salem, but Daisy told her to be grateful.

Jay had decided about two years back that my scribbling had grown regionally famous enough to merit rewarding with a vessel. It better have done, I'd pointed out at the time, seeing as it was mainly *my* profits that were going to foot the refurbishment bill.

"Mother, I'm running away," Pam said, turning to Daisy. "I'm going to come live with Uncle Nick and read his entire library. Jay's going to teach me how to sail."

"Not if you know what's good for you, precious," Daisy replied. "You know you're all set to take a place at the Spence School this fall. You need to learn some manners."

"Well, that's handy," said Pam, defiantly, pitching over to lean beside me against the railing. "Spence is in New York, isn't it? There are plenty of trains to Boston."

"You'd better go to school," I told her. "None of the colleges will accept you otherwise. But you're welcome to come up here on weekends. I'll even send a car if you like."

"No, I'll take the train," Pam insisted, her smile widening in the face of her mother's barely concealed horror. "I *like* trains. They're very romantic. Aren't they, Jay?"

Intent at the ropes, Jay hummed noncommittally, but he was smiling.

"College?" Daisy echoed warily. "Who said anything about college?"

"I did," Pam told her. "People up here believe girls have got brains."

"You'll never get a husband that way. A clever girl is a single girl."

"Then I hope I'm a regular genius," said Pam, leaning against my shoulder.

Backed by that impossible expanse of sky, Jay was watching us with his usual intense gravity. I loved him all the more for it—and, much to my delight, I loved Pam, too.

CHAPTER 5

Better Than Boys

P am came to stay with us the weekend before starting at Spence. Daisy had rung ahead of time, so fed up with her daughter's pestering in the scant few months since their visit that she'd told us we were welcome to backtrack with her down to New York and see her off ourselves.

When I asked her what Tom thought about that, she said, "Mind your own damn business, Nicky. Our life isn't free material for your next gossip column."

I didn't tell her it had been the subject of so much more, albeit nothing published.

"Forget I asked," I said instead. "What time does Pam's train get into South Station?"

"Late afternoon," Daisy said, rummaging around in what sounded like slips of paper.

"Trains have specific times," I reminded her. "Did you write down that information?"

There was some more rummaging, and then Daisy's gasp of triumph. "Four o'clock."

"We'll be there," I promised. "Are there any particular considerations or requests?"

"I'd say don't spoil her," Daisy retorted, "but neither of you would listen anyway." She paused, seemingly thoughtful. "Neither of you ever struck me as fond of children."

"Well, you learn something strange and new every day," I said. "So do we."

"You didn't used to think you were clever. The fame's gone to your head."

"*Some* level of wit is required to write competently. That's how it works."

Daisy huffed. "You're more than competent, Nicky. We both know it."

That was the first compliment Daisy had paid me in quite a long time.

"Then I hope you're satisfied that Pam's in good intellectual hands."

"I gave up on hoping she wouldn't be smart a long time ago. What worries me is the . . . *social* example you two are going to set for her impressionable young mind."

"If you'd really been afraid of that, you wouldn't have brought her here in the first place," I said, unsurprised, given the compliments couldn't last. "That's just lip service. Either that or it's Tom talking, and you know we don't give a damn about what he thinks."

"You give a damn about Pammy," Daisy said. "I'll just have to console myself with that."

"Somebody's got to," I replied, fed up with the sound of her voice. "Goodbye, Daisy."

When I related the conversation to Jay, he remarked, "That's alarming, isn't it?"

"Yes and no." I sighed, joining him at the table for a lunch of cold leftovers.

"Sounds like you need to get it out of your system, old sport," Jay coaxed.

Down the years, that nickname had become nothing shy of an endearment.

"Jay, she's worried about the *social example* we'll set. She sounds just like my father commenting on, what was it—my *questionable proclivities*. You need to look no further for proof my whole family's got a way with words. It's just very often a *dubious* way."

Jay chewed a bite of his sandwich and then chewed his lip. "I overheard some of what you two talked about when we were at Harvard.

I wouldn't want to get caught in the crossfire when you and Daisy go at it. I've seen exchanges of bullets more civil."

"I never fought my father the way I fight her," I admitted, troubled.

"That points to either respect for your elders, a lack of respect for women, or both."

"Neither of us has been what you'd call good at the latter. Look at our track record."

"We can make amends. Our interactions with Pam have been a start, don't you think?"

I picked at the pickles on the side of my plate. "That means being kinder to Daisy."

"What kind of person you are doesn't depend upon sex," Jay pointed out. "Daisy's a rotten person, and so is Tom. I'd no sooner be more than passing polite to either of them. And if Daisy had laid into me the same way she laid into you . . . "

"That's not entirely fair to her," I said grudgingly. "I've been the instigator just as often."

"If you feel strongly about it, the solution's either to hold your tongue or not talk to her," Jay concluded. "We're going to be seeing a lot of Pam, so the latter might be moot."

"You give better advice than you used to," I said in admiration, giving up on the pickles, handing them over to him. "Sometimes, you even practice what you preach."

A week later, full of jittery but overjoyed anticipation, Jay and I went to meet Pam. Her train ran thirty minutes late, which meant we spent a lot of time sharing smokes and flipping through various pieces of questionable literature at the newsstand.

We rushed to the track as soon as the tardy four o'clock was announced, out of breath.

"Jay! Uncle Nick!" Pam shouted, dashing toward us full tilt, leaving the baggage attendant she had hired far behind her. "I thought Mother would *never* let me come back!"

Even though I staggered worse than the first time Pam had thrown herself into my arms, I held on like before. She was even taller than

I remembered, now able to look me straight in the eye. Did children always grow that fast? Maybe teenagers did, and I just didn't remember.

"Hasn't been that long; don't be dramatic," Jay said, grinning as Pam finally released me and turned to him. "What's your mother's kitchen staff been feeding you, anyway?"

"*I'm* dramatic?" Pam scoffed, punching Jay's shoulder. "Don't be a wet sock!"

Jay clapped her arm in return, clearing his throat. "I've sure missed you, and your uncle Nick can say the same. A regular pair of broken records. You'll get sick of hearing it."

Pam waved him off, cheerfully embarrassed. "You mean a pair of wet socks!"

The baggage attendant looked even more scandalized at that exchange than he had at Pam's exuberant sprint. I helped him unload her luggage, tipped him, and said he could leave.

"You'll have to explain the sock parlance," I said once we were outside the station.

"Means the same thing as a stick in the mud," Jay clarified. "An unpopular person."

"Jay hears a lot of things down at the docks, I bet," Pam said. "Teach me to swear?"

"I'll teach you no such thing," Jay cautioned. "But sure, I can't keep you from overhearing. Those young ears of yours are sharp," he added and then winked.

On getting home, we discovered that Pam's luggage occupied most of our narrow entryway. Before Jay could offer to help her haul it upstairs, she dragged three of her suitcases into the sitting room, opened them, and pitched half of the contents haphazardly onto the nearest armchair. She repacked her remaining items in the largest suitcase of the three.

"I'm leaving that stuff here," Pam explained, pointing to the perilous mound on the armchair. "That bureau and the closet in the spare room are empty, right?" She glanced imploringly at Jay and then at me. "Don't tell Mother. She'd have a fit if she found out."

"I don't see any harm in it," I said jovially, mostly so Jay would relax in spite of what she'd just foisted on us. "She expects you'll be coming here for the occasional visit anyway."

Jay waited until Pam had gathered up the ungainly armload and vanished upstairs.

"That amount of stuff is more than just occasional," he said uneasily. "I should know."

"What are you afraid of?" I asked, taking hold of the two empty suitcases. "Daisy?"

"Not for my own sake," Jay said, grabbing the repacked one. "For Pam's, though . . . "

"Tom's a brute, but he dotes on Pam," I reassured him. "He'd never hurt her."

"Not physically, no," Jay relented, following me to the staircase. "I'd hope not."

Once Pam had settled in, we took her to one of our old haunts for dinner. The Parker House Hotel had been demolished and rebuilt in twenty-seven. Now, the Omni Parker House stood even swankier than before, retaining its stately presence across from the Common.

"You talked about this place the first time I was here," Pam said, her mouth full of cream pie since she'd impishly ordered dessert first. "We walked past it with Mother. She wanted to go inside and see the lobby. You said *later*," she imitated my sternness, "and then we didn't."

I glanced at Jay in the event he wanted to explain. Sometimes letting him control the level of detail about what others learned or *didn't* learn about our history was the best course.

"Your uncle and I stayed here when we got back from Europe," Jay said, stealing a bite of Pam's dessert. "We called it home till we bought the house, you see. Fond memories."

"Get your own!" Pam exclaimed, but she pushed the plate toward the middle of the table. "And I *do* see. It was after your . . . " She hesitated. "Is this a popular place for honeymoons?"

"It's popular for weddings," I said. "You hear jazz almost every night in the summer."

Pam gave me a sad sort of look, tilting her chin up. "Maybe some-day," she said, which was heartbreakingly clever. Anyone listening would think she meant her own eventual nuptials.

"You'd have to book now, groom unseen," Jay said. "As for a hon-eymoon, it would suit."

"There was a pamphlet in the lobby," Pam said, tactfully changing the subject. "The front said Charles Dickens stayed here while he was performing *Christmas Carol*. The first time was right here in the hotel, even. Writers back then were so glamorous."

"So I heard," I admitted. "He lived here, more like. This city ate it up."

Pam tipped her chin back down, glaring at me from beneath her lashes. "You don't like Dickens, Uncle Nick?" She appealed to Jay, her eyes gentling. "Is he a Scrooge all winter?"

"No, he's quite fond of snow. I am, too. You have to remember where we're from."

"Mother says she's glad her branch of the family ended up some-where warmer."

I could have said any number of things about Louisville based on the times I'd gone to visit Daisy and Tom, but none of them were ring-ing endorsements. I opted for finishing Pam's cream pie while Jay told her more about Parker House history. The maître d' looked impatient when he arrived to ask for our main course selections. I told him.

Two hours later, once we were finished, I settled the tab. The maître d' was relieved to be rid of us. We filed out into the blue dusk and cut uphill across the Common to get home. No one cared if Pam and Jay went on chattering. For the entirety of the walk, I was con-tent to listen.

"You showed a lot of restraint, old sport," Jay declared once Pam had gone to bed.

"What, at dinner?" I asked lightly. "You two gave me no choice. Thick as thieves."

"Usually, it's all I can do to keep you from dwelling on what's behind us."

"We've made a life here, Jay. I have fewer reasons to do that all the time."

"Thanks for sparing us the Louisville rant. She might've gotten mine, too."

Pensive, I leaned back into his arm, where it was draped across the sofa. Louisville represented faux civil society and an unsavory past. People like Tom existed everywhere, but I'd never run into as many here as I did there. That branch of the family tree, over-adorned with orchids and bougainvillea, was an embarrassment even to the likes of my father.

"Penny for your thoughts?" Jay prompted, tightening his arm around my shoulders.

"It wasn't all bad, was it?" I ventured. "New York, the *city itself*—that part went sour for me. But when I think about West Egg, the mansion and the cottage, can be . . . nostalgic."

"Castle Rackrent is the stuff of dreams," Jay said, and we laughed till our sides hurt.

Taking Pam back to South Station at the end of the week was harder than it should have been. Jay had taken her sailing every day the wind had been good enough, and I'd taken her into the office to meet my co-workers and shuffle through drafts of my columns spanning the better part of the last decade. Everyone had been charmed with her, especially the co-worker whose name I had finally learned. He was charming, occasionally insolent, and went by Tom.

"I'll call twice a week," Pam promised, doing her best to put on a brave face.

"Will they let you use the phone that often?" I asked. "Boarding schools can be strict. I never went to one, but plenty of the fellows I knew at Yale did. I heard stories."

"I can find a phone when I need one," Pam said haughtily. "I have my ways."

"You're the most resourceful young lady I've ever met," Jay told her earnestly. "You're going to get on just fine in New York. Plenty of opportunities for a clever girl like you."

Pam was smiling, but something resembling doubt flashed in her glance. There were moments in which she reminded me of the effigies she'd loved—those sad, round eyes.

"If I ever need to call you for something more serious, Uncle Nick, can I?"

"What in the world do you mean by serious? They'll take good care of you."

"I mean if there's any trouble. It's not very likely, but . . . I'd feel better."

Jay sensed my perplexity and stepped in. "You can call us for any reason."

"Okay," Pam said, brightening, and threw her arms around each of us in turn. "Goodbye, Jay and Uncle Nick. Thank you for everything. Wish you could come down with me!"

"Maybe next time," I said, my throat tight as she dashed off to meet her train.

That evening at home, I couldn't stop circling back to what Pam had asked. Could she call me about something more serious? Where had she gotten it into her head that she might need to do a thing like that? Was there anything Daisy hadn't told me? I stewed like that in the armchair until Jay nudged my elbow and handed me an Old Fashioned.

"She'll get there just fine," he said. "Trains tend to be reliable."

"That's not it," I said, drinking deeply. "It's what she asked."

"Kids her age worry, especially when they have leisure to."

"Don't think badly of me for saying this, but I wonder if there's something Daisy didn't tell me. We've only seen the side of her that's sweetness and light. There could be more."

"If she'd been acting out, Daisy would've said something. She'd want us to iron habits out of Pam that might risk the family reputation. She'd sooner listen to you than her mother."

"She'd sooner listen to *you* than me," I said bluntly.

Jay stuck his hands in his pockets and went to the sofa.

"If you think this is a contest, Nick, please reconsider."

"I don't," I said earnestly. "But what if it comes to that?"

"Comes to what? I'm afraid I don't follow."

"To Pam acting out. Needing discipline."

Jay looked thoroughly miserable at the prospect, but he said, "That's a valid concern."

"What happened to your confidence in Daisy sharing information?" I replied warily.

"Something occurred to me," Jay admitted. "She's been with governesses all her life."

"So . . . *Christ.*" I drank for courage. "If there are problems, Daisy might not know."

Jay nodded. "Exactly. We'll just have to play it by ear. Do our best to keep tabs."

"Forget her calling us twice a week," I said bitterly. "I'll have to restrain myself from calling the headmistress daily. I'll get fired for misuse of the company phone line."

"Let's not borrow trouble, Nick. I just . . . want to be prepared."

It was one of those profound moments in which I couldn't help but marvel at how far Jay had come since we first met. I knew that I'd come just as far, but Jay's admirable qualities had tripled where mine had only doubled if I was fortunate. I joined him on the sofa.

"I couldn't do this alone," I said. "I'm grateful Pam has you."

"If you were alone, you know what that'd imply about me."

"We're alive, Jay. We're alive, we're here, and one of Daisy's mistakes is finally worth fixing." I regretted saying that almost instantly. "Not to imply Pam is the mistake."

"No, no," Jay said. "The mistake is her parents' hands-off, *ah*—parenting."

"I don't understand it," I went on. "I wasn't fobbed off on household staff, but heaven knows my parents could afford it. Maybe it's cultural. Still, I feel the South's been terrible for that branch of the family. I don't know any of my family in Saint Paul and Chicago who—"

"I don't give a damn about what the rest do," Jay said. "What *you* do matters."

Feeling scattered, I finished my drink. "How did we get to this point, Jay? How?"

"You let me talk you into being decent," Jay said fondly. "When the letter came."

"Says more about your character than mine," I protested. "You just needed . . . "

"Traditionally, I've taken all the wrong opportunities. This one seemed right."

My head on his shoulder, I nodded, not about to contradict the love of my life.

◆──◇══◇──◇

The week before term let out for the Thanksgiving holiday, Pam called me at work, her voice on the line instantly recognizable. There hadn't been a soul in my office all morning, not even Tom. She sounded so bored and forlorn that it made my pre-existing tendency toward procrastination all the easier to indulge. I asked her if everything was all right.

"Uncle Nick," Pam began ominously, "I'm in an awful lot of trouble."

My conspiratorial hopes for the call turned instantly to subdued panic. Either something unforeseen had truly happened, or there was a reason she had asked if she could call us. The former meant emergency; the latter meant premeditation. Neither option was reassuring.

"Whatever it is," I said, forcing my voice steady, "it can't be worse than what your father got up to at college. He dragged me into his schemes. Neither of us got expelled."

"Did you ever try that Harvard prank, the one with a cow in the dean's office?"

I was puzzled by the conversation's turn. If she was thinking about trying her hand at a shenanigan or two, there were any number of trivial ones she could attempt.

"That's apocryphal. Streaking across campus during winter was popular, though."

"Well," Pam said, relaxing into a drawl, "I pulled a prank on the headmistress."

I covered my mouth, leaning hard with both elbows against my desk. "Oh?"

"I couldn't find a cow," Pam went on. "Her office is on the ground floor, so it would've defeated the purpose. Caroline says the reason you have to lead it up some stairs is so it won't go back down. Anyway, we put our heads together and decided chickens would work."

I bit the flesh of my palm, hyperventilating for a few moments in sheer relief.

"How did you get the chickens into her office? Don't they lock it at night?"

"I *hoped* you'd understand," Pam said happily. "She leaves a window open. We slashed the screen, shoved the birds through, and then taped it shut again."

"How many chickens? Where did you even *get* them?"

"Fowler Avenue Market in Flushing. We bought four."

"How much trouble can you really get into with chickens?"

"They shat on everything. I'm being sent home early."

"For break or for the whole year?" I asked, uneasy again.

"For break," Pam huffed. "But I can't call Mother."

I scrubbed at my eyes with both hands, sighing. If Pam was anything like her father, then she took after him in that she possessed a bold and restless sense of mischief. I would have been lying to claim that I hadn't enjoyed getting dragged along on Tom's various escapades.

"Didn't they call her for you?" I asked, bewildered. "I thought that was standard."

"They're probably calling Jay as we speak," Pam admitted guilt-ily. "I told them Mother was visiting at yours. Besides, Headmistress Clanchy is as tight-fisted as they come. New York to Boston's a cheaper call than New York to Alexandria."

I could only imagine what Jay must have been making of the phone call with Clanchy.

"You can come here for a week. We won't tell your mother you're not at school, but we're sending you home for Thanksgiving proper. You're going to have to get subtler."

"About pranks?" Pam asked hopefully. "You'll have to tell me some clever ones."

When I got home, Jay was in the back garden splitting logs for the fireplace. He set aside the ax when he heard me approach, brushing his hands off. His expression was pinched.

"I'm sorry you had to take that call," I said. "Meanwhile, Pam called me at work."

"It was all I could do," Jay sighed, "realizing I had to agree that Daisy was here."

I stepped closer under the guise of brushing off his shirt. "I told her she could come here for a week. After that, I made her promise to spend the holiday at home."

"She could've been expelled," Jay said reproachfully. "And then—"

"We'd never see her," I replied, sharing in his upset. "Jay, I know."

"Pam's train gets in late." Jay sighed. "It's been a hard day, old sport."

"You should rest," I said, reassured when he leaned into me. "I'll go."

In the days immediately following, Pam got her first real taste of discipline under our roof. I begged off work for a week, fortunate that Taylor had faith in my ability to meet deadlines from home. Pam was cross that I'd appointed myself as her tutor, but she seemed to resign herself to the fact she wouldn't be permitted to bum around the Seaport District with Jay.

About the time I caught her smoking one of my cigarettes in the greenhouse when she was meant to be getting some fresh air, all I could do was give in and join her. She lit the Sobranie dangling from her lip with Jay's old trench lighter and then lit mine for me.

"What are we going to do with you?" I asked, blowing smoke at the overcast sky.

Pam shivered, taking a deep drag. "Help me keep out of trouble," she exhaled, turning the cigarette between her fingers. "Black wrappers? These are fancy."

"I'm serious, Pam," I went on. "We can't cover for you every time."

Nodding dejectedly, Pam looked away from me. "Sure, I know that."

"If you get expelled from Spence, we'll never see you," I sighed.

"Is that you talking or Jay talking?" Pam asked, suddenly curious.

"That's both of us talking. You should've heard us, regular saps."

"That's old news. I'm touched, though. Mother would just . . . I don't know, find me another new school and hand Daddy the bill," Pam said, chagrined. "I just . . . wanted to know."

"Wanted to know what?" I asked, wishing Jay was there to hear what came next.

"That somebody cares," Pam said simply. "I'm never sure about Mother. She talks a good game, but I had governesses till I was ten. Daddy would buy the moon if I asked, but . . . "

"But?" I prompted, dropping my unfinished cigarette onto the frost-wilted grass.

"He's not like you and Uncle Jay," Pam said, pitching what was left of hers, too.

"Thanks," I managed. "Say, have you . . . "

"Called Jay that to his face? No. Not yet."

"You should," I told her. "Let's go inside."

That night, over dinner, Pam took my advice. She made it sound so casual that Jay didn't appear to realize what had come out of her mouth until she'd finished talking about her lessons.

"I'm proud of you asking for help, dear heart," he said, misty-eyed. "I truly am."

After the week was up, we saw Pam off on her train to Virginia. I was more stoic than Jay, who fretted about her absence. We had a few friends of ours over for Thanksgiving dinner, although Tom from the office had declined. They joked about us empty nesting.

Daisy didn't find out about Pam's close call, although part of me wished I could fling it in her careless face. Jay knew what was in my heart of hearts because it was in his, too.

◆━━▽━━◆

Much to Jay's unabashed relief and mine, Pam made it to winter break without risking expulsion. There was always the possibility that she'd pulled another prank and not gotten caught, but during the few days she was set to spend with us before heading home to Virginia, I was determined not to ask. I couldn't remember the last time I'd been part of a proper family Christmas, and Jay said the ones he remembered growing up hadn't been all that festive.

Daisy called while Pam was on her way up to us by way of the customary train. Her motivations for reaching out felt like they'd changed. I could never tell if she rang because she wanted to fluster me, or if she was genuinely concerned for Pam, or if she was just lonely.

"You better not get her too many gifts to transport home and then back to school."

"The gifts have already been bought," I informed her. "Most of them will stay here."

Daisy sounded like she was smoking. "I shudder to think how much clutter she's left in your upstairs. That house is cozy, don't get me wrong—but it's awfully small."

"Are you implying that you don't like the fact Pam has basically moved in, or that we should buy a bigger house? Jay and I have done well for ourselves, but not *that* well."

Daisy's silence on the other end of the line had a different feel to it than the other times she'd decided to make me squirm. Her breathing had taken on a labored quality that might have meant she was desperate to finish her cigarette. I found out quickly that was *not* the case.

"Let's get one thing straight, Nicky," Daisy snapped. "Pammy's *my* daughter."

"I never said she wasn't," I replied defensively, which made Jay raise his eyebrows as he walked into the room. "Nobody here is trying to take your place."

"Could have fooled me," Daisy retorted. "You and Jay think you're better than Tom and me, don't you, because she'd rather spend time up there than at home."

Jay was frozen on the spot, straining to listen. Daisy's voice had grown so loud that he could probably catch every other word. I beckoned him over to the phone, holding the receiver out from my ear so that he could listen in on the remainder of the call with greater ease.

"I never said anything like that, either," I told Daisy. "Where'd you get the idea—"

"*Tom* got the idea. He's the one talking for once. I felt like a fool when he made me realize how far gone Pammy was on you, Nicky."

"Wait a minute," Jay said, sounding mad for the first time in years. "I can't help but notice you said gone on *Nick*. Does Tom even know who this *Jay* is that your cousin lives with?"

Daisy made a hurt sound, and we heard her lighter's frantic *click.* "Let's not remind him."

"How'd he agree to let Pam stay here on the regular if he knew who it was?" I asked.

"If you weren't so convenient, it'd be a totally different story. Count your blessings."

For the first time since we'd regularly begun talking on the phone, I hung up on her without saying goodbye. Jay gave me an approving nod, otherwise too angry to comment.

"You're both very quiet," Pam chided on the way back to ours from South Station.

"We had the misfortune of an unpleasant conversation earlier today," Jay said dully.

Pam was shocked and then upset as she looked at me. "*Please* don't tell me you fought."

"The conversation was with your mother," I explained. "She made false accusations."

In spite of her relief, Pam was furious. "That's *rotten*. What did she say?"

"That we're trying to steal you away," Jay replied. "That's patently untrue."

"She also asked us not to get you too many gifts," I added, "but it's too late."

Pam was gleeful about the gift revelation, but her expression clouded again in no time at all. She looked exactly like her mother did when she was winding up to say something cruel.

"I wish you *were* trying to steal me," she said vehemently and then burst into tears.

The cabbie didn't so much as give us a second glance in the rear-view mirror. Like his New York counterparts, he'd seen everything under the sun, bouts of crying included.

We were only a few minutes from home, so I did my best to console Pam until we got there. She had only one suitcase this time, so it was easy for Jay to spirit that upstairs while I sat Pam down at the kitchen table. We had Mélange Hédiard, which she loved, too, so I made some.

"I know you're angry with your mother," I said, realizing I'd have to be convincing about what came next, "but you shouldn't say that. She cares for you even if she's misguided."

Jay came into the kitchen and joined us, claiming the tea I'd made for him.

"Don't patronize me," Pam sniffled into her mug, slurping loudly. "*Liar.*"

"Which part of what he said are you calling a lie, exactly?" Jay pressed.

"You *know* what part, Uncle Jay. Mother doesn't care. She never cared about you, she never cared about Uncle Nick, and she *definitely* never cared about me!"

I was too stunned to react. I wanted to say that I agreed with every word, but the price was too high. Pam's presence in our life was a gift Daisy and Tom could take away. They'd whisk her out of the country at a moment's notice if we outlived our convenience.

Pam spent the next few minutes gulping her tea, clutching Jay's hand until it was bloodless against the table. By the time she was done, she'd stopped crying. She looked at me.

"You don't have to say anything," Pam said quietly. "I can't afford to lose you, either."

"Nobody's going to lose anybody," Jay replied. "We're going to have ourselves the merriest Christmas there ever was, and there's not a damn thing Daisy can do about it."

That last part, he said for my benefit as much as for Pam's, and I was comforted.

"Oh, all these bells!" said Pam, radiant with amazement. "Uncle Nick, just *listen.*"

The three of us occupied a little bench near the hedge maze in Notre-Dame Cathedral's garden. As none of us were Catholic, the Good Friday clamor was perhaps, symbolically, a touch lost. Pam removed her hat and scooted forward, face tilted upward, knees daringly exposed. Her pale hair scarcely brushed her earlobes, which sported dangling pearls.

"I'm no churchgoer, but if I was, I'd content myself with these *any* Sunday," I told her, but she was already lost in an ecstatic, sound-swept world of her own.

A year and a half on from Pam's poultry-fueled escapade, this particular trip had been Jay's idea. We'd taken Pam to Canada during her spring break the year before, retracing our steps through Montréal and Québec City. Pending good behavior, Jay had promised we'd take her to Europe as a sequel. From January through to term's end just the week before, her conduct had been pristine. Headmistress Clanchy was no doubt suspicious.

"Kind of place you'd want for weddings and funerals," Jay said. "Very proper."

"There you go," Pam teased, elbowing his ribs. "On about weddings again."

At the thought of funerals, my blood ran cold. It felt ominous enough, facing the prospect of Jay's forty-fourth birthday and my forty-second soon after. We were fortunate, said Tom at the office, not to have many gray hairs between us. He and his housemate, Amory—as much his husband as Jay was mine, or so I had gathered by implication—had only a few years on us. Tom loudly lamented that they were beginning to suffer the salt-and-pepper scourges of time.

I told him once that it felt strange to like someone called Tom after the first person I'd known by that name had so thoroughly sullied it. Tom had suggested the four of us have drinks sometime. I told him Jay and I would like that but that we should steer clear of Causeway Street.

Tom said Amory might take winning over, having grown cautious of the bottle after indiscretions in his youth, but the promise of meeting a journalist-turned-novelist whose début he greatly admired ought to do the trick. I rubbed my neck in consternation, no gesture of false modesty, thinking of my *actual* first manuscript under lock and key in the cellar.

"Not *my* wedding," said Pam with sober decisiveness. "I shan't be having one."

"You're fortunate enough that you'll be able to afford independence," I conceded.

"You never know, dear heart," Jay said, somehow the only person on earth who got away with calling her endearments just shy of

Daisy's *precious*. "You might fall for someone. If that happens, you'll have a decision to make. If you're lucky, you'll meet an Ivy Leaguer or an Oxford man who knows the value of a fine and educated young lady."

Pam's eyes were fixed on the grass now instead of the sky, her hands folded.

"Even if I did," she said hesitantly, "I'm pretty sure that he wouldn't want me."

Exchanging concerned glances with Jay, I put a tentative arm around her.

"What in the world makes you say that? *Anyone* would be lucky to have you."

"Do you remember those doctor's appointments right after New Year's?" asked Pam, her restless eyes hard and glittering. "The ones Mother had me telling you were all about measuring my growth. I mean, since now I'm taller than Aunt Jordan? Well, that's a lie. It's just rotten of me not to have said anything. There's a . . . " She hesitated, glancing first at Jay, as if to make sure he hadn't lost his sympathy, and then at me, with a cutting sincerity that only blood kin with a common grievance could impart. "There's a problem," she said quietly. "With me. Inside. Something's not right, or gone funny, or . . . I can't get Mother to tell me what it is. The doctor won't tell me no matter how I turn on the tears, or . . . "

"Take all the time you need," I prompted gently.

"Look, I don't mean to be crude, but I think something's missing. They poke me and prod me like I'm one of those cadavers at Yale Medical School like Daddy used to talk about at Halloween. Uncle Nick, I don't—I don't *bleed*. I shouldn't like books more than boys!"

Jay responded first by squeezing her hand. He looked helpless, woefully out of his depth, but in the way he did when he thought he was hiding it.

Mercifully, Pam was far too upset to take notice.

My mind whirled, thoughts scrabbling at the edge of a memory that I couldn't pin down. I was almost positive it had something to do with Tom and Yale, although I couldn't put my finger on why that was. The string of associations it set off was anything but reassuring.

"I liked books better than girls at your age. For that matter," I said, lowering my voice so that passersby wouldn't hear, "I probably liked them better than boys, too. Or anything else."

"They want to cut me open this summer," said Pam numbly. "Just to see."

"Barbaric," Jay said, and then added: "Surely your father won't allow it."

"Uncle Jay," Pam lamented, tears beginning to fall, "Daddy doesn't *know*."

That was when the memory clicked into place. Tom Buchanan and I had once spent a drunken evening in the Yale boathouse with a clutch of medical students, *also* drunk, over tomes full of what they termed *deviant* case studies. Those pages held the revelation of details to which the patients surely hadn't consented. Tom had been repelled; ashamed, I hadn't said a word.

Pam had her father's quick eyes and decisive jaw, but the latter was slightly softened.

"I got the head nurse at school to sneak me some books. She didn't prod me the same way Mother's doctor does, with . . . " She shook her head, and what she *didn't* say gave me the first urge I'd ever had to punch someone's lights out. "She's been at Spence for forty years. She said there was a girl like me in ought-seven. Tall, too, and no monthlies."

One afternoon on lunch break at the Yale Club in New York, after failing to read about finance, my eyes had fallen on what I recognized as one of the medical texts from the boathouse. I flipped through it, eventually landing on an illustrative figure. *Subject with XY chromosomal pattern and phenotypic developmental anomaly, i.e., pseudo-hermaphrodite.*

The language of that caption was so peculiar, yet so specific, that I hadn't forgotten after happening across it a second time. The probable relevance of it shook me.

"You're not worth any less," I told Pam. "You're just different. Do you understand?"

"I can't have children, and I want to kiss Caroline," she whispered. "What do I *do*?"

"Whatever you damned well want," Jay said, leaning close. "You're richer than God."

Pam's eyes lit up shrewdly beneath her tears, as if he'd flipped some kind of switch.

"Whatever I want with *whomever* I want, like Gladys Bentley at the Ubangi?" she asked, and, from the mention of a popular jazz club, I presumed Ms. Bentley was a performer known for keeping female company. "I want that to be true. Do you really think so?"

"Dear heart," Jay said, tenderly brushing her pale, damp cheek, "I *know* so."

We got back to Boston three days before Pam was due back at school. Once we'd all bathed, had a full night's sleep, and eaten breakfast, I phoned Daisy while Jay distracted Pam with the most complex knot-tying exercises he could devise.

"It's not right, what you plan to do to Pam," I said, without the courtesy of a greeting. "Whatever it's called, whatever she's got, it's not life-threatening. People like her lead normal lives. All the time, Daisy—till they're treated like lab specimens. What were you *thinking*?"

"Tell it to her father, Nicky," Daisy challenged. "You tell Tom his baby girl's got the wrong parts in the wrong place. Hell, tell him his baby girl should've been a baby *boy*." She took a shaky breath, and I imagined the curl of her cigarette smoke toward the arched, elegant ceiling. "He's got to think she's having her appendix out. Doctor Bennett says that's the only way."

"You're not letting them operate," I said, "because she's not coming home."

"I *beg* your pardon?" snapped Daisy coldly. "So it's come to this, has it?"

"She's hardly ever home anyway, and she gets into all kinds of trouble at school. Did you know that? You'd just as soon run around with Jordan while Tom sees senators' wives on the sly. It'd be the most convenient thing that ever happened to you, Daisy. Jay and I have never been more useful than we are now. If you refuse, I'll see to it *your* ghosts rise."

The silence that fell between us over the distance and the wire was profound, unholy.

"It . . . it would be for her own good," said Daisy, already feigning martyrdom. "That way, Tom need never find out. By the time she's through college, she'll have met somebody. I guess *he* need not ever know she's barren till he's been married to her for years."

"You'll send her money," I told Daisy sternly, "and keep her in the will. We can afford custody, don't get me wrong, but you brought her into this world. That carries a price."

"Tell me, Nicky—is she what you always wanted, or what you always wanted to *be*?"

"Goodbye, Daisy," I said and hung up. My family was waiting for me in the kitchen.

CHAPTER 6

Love and War

P am took the news with scarcely contained joy, which cemented my resolve never to speak with Daisy again if I could help it. Our phone calls concerning Pam's schooling and travel felt like more camaraderie than I ever should have allowed. Knowing those exchanges had been necessary only helped insofar as they had permitted Jay and me to offer Pam peace and safety.

Never speaking with Tom again had been a foregone conclusion, and I was positive the feeling was mutual. There was always the possibility Daisy hadn't told him the whole truth about the man I was living with in Boston, but our conversation at Christmas had disabused me of that notion. Swearing an exuberant Pam to secrecy after that first visit wouldn't have been possible.

Pam had entered Spence as an eighth-grader shortly after she first came to see us in the fall of 1932. We had wondered at the time why Pam's school in Virginia had forced her out after seventh grade. Daisy had implied that she wanted Pam in an institution more akin to finishing school. Now, in light of the pranks, we knew what that reference to *manners* had really meant.

With spring break of 1933 having been spent in Canada and spring break of 1934 having been spent in France—*and* with Pam moving in permanently after the latter trip—we abruptly realized Pam would be entering her sophomore year come fall. Pam's ongoing inconsistent levels of studiousness at Spence prompted me to inquire about suitable schools closer to home.

Headmaster Hapgood at Girls' Latin wasn't about to shy from Pam's record—or, we supposed, from the guaranteed tuition she brought with her. While I would like to claim that Pam's acting out stopped altogether, the truth is that, with the start of her sophomore year in Boston and no further need for boarding, it merely receded to a less obtrusive pitch.

Simply put, Pam missed Caroline. They exchanged sporadic letters throughout the fall of 1934, but in the spring of 1935, Pam's paramour stopped writing altogether. Jay and I counted ourselves fortunate that no Bronx matron had come knocking on our door with an eye toward raining retribution on Pam for corrupting her daughter. Nonetheless, Pam was disconsolate, and no amount of bribery by sailing trip could put a stop to Pam's last spate of pranks.

"Look on the bright side, old sport," Jay said about a month after school let out for the summer, finally showing a touch of gray at the temples. "She never did get her hands on a cow."

"She's more likely to find one here than in New York," I replied. "Don't push your luck."

We delayed our customary travel until July, only revealing to Pam at the last minute what passage I had booked for the three of us this time. She attempted to swallow the thrill, composing her sun-browned features, but her windswept blond bob still lent an air of girlish excitement to what was now otherwise *undeniably* a young woman's visage.

"Well, London was the only place left," Pam said airily, giving in to a grin at last. She kicked her work boots off next to Jay's at the back door. "That and Oxford."

"We'll make stops all over," I reassured her. "Wherever else you like."

"I never made it to Ireland," Jay remarked, sipping coffee at the table.

"I never made it to Ireland *or* Scotland," I said. "My ancestors came from both. My father never liked to admit it, but anything Scots-Irish got jumbled once it hopped the pond."

"Mother always said her side and yours was Scottish," Pam replied, "but all I could find for Carraway was Irish. Maybe that's why you like this city so much?"

I gave Pam a good-naturedly withering glance, but Jay outright roared with hilarity.

"Buchanan's Scottish," Pam said at length, waving him off. "I looked it up once."

"Gatz is your garden variety German to Slavic," Jay replied. "Nothing to see here."

Just as I opened my mouth to say I had once researched *Gatsby* back to its origins as a tenth-century Norse transplant to England, something fantastical occurred to me. Pam had never so much as heard her parents speak that name. She had never heard it from Jay or me, either.

"Anyway, you'd better start packing," I told her instead. "We leave in a week."

Jay followed me out to the greenhouse with what was left of his cold coffee.

"I know that look. You're feeling guilty about something you haven't done."

"Fine," I said, making sure the pages of my latest column were secured under the heavy, flat beach stone that Pam had labeled NEXT WEEK'S RAG in black marker. "I almost said it."

Given our surname discussion, it didn't take Jay long to discern what I meant. "*Nick*."

Shaking my head, I hit a few keys on the empty typewriter. "Didn't say I was proud."

"She can never know," Jay said, teeth clenched. "For her protection as much as ours!"

"Well, thank God those old shirts of yours she wears are only monogrammed JG!"

"Stop whispering out there!" Pam called. "Cat's out of the bag; we're going to Blighty!"

As soon as she went back inside, I shook my head. "We can't shelter her forever."

"No, but we can make sure she never has cause to hate us like she hates her parents."

"She's smart and stubborn. If she ever decides we haven't shared enough of our past—"

"If you don't get in here, I'll make food for one instead of three!" Pam yelled.

"It's not your night to cook!" Jay shouted back. "It's your Uncle Nick's turn!"

All throughout dinner, I struggled to put the conversation out of my mind. I tried to remember if my dusty searches in the *Globe's* basement archive had turned up any coverage mentioning the name Gatsby. Years had passed since the attempt. I concluded that I must not have found anything, instead lingering over happier thoughts of impending travel.

Knowing full well the flights of fancy that Jay and Pam were likely to indulge, leaving me no option but to be happily whisked along, I made sure we had nearly twice as long on the ground as we had on our previous trips. If five weeks wasn't enough for the entirety of England, Scotland, and Ireland, then we were in for more unplanned detours than I could imagine.

Traveling by ship wasn't unfamiliar to Pam, as she had crossed the Atlantic half a dozen times with her parents by the age of twelve. What was novel to her was having a cabin that she didn't have to share with an overly attentive nanny. She raved about the bed being more comfortable than the one in her room at home, unsubtly hinting that she wanted a new one.

Jay and I saw little enough of her during the five-day voyage that we managed to relive that particular sliver of our glory days. Jay's scars bothered him more than they used to, and my back hurt from long days seated at a desk. Obtrusive though they were, these conditions were more the subject of amusement than grief. We'd come to prefer intimacy that included mirth.

After making port, Pam realized I hadn't told her where in London we were staying. She'd studied the city's geography, but not thoroughly enough to determine where the hackney was taking us until we'd been dropped off at Claridge's in Mayfair.

"I was hoping for the Ritz or the Grosvenor," Pam teased as the bellhop with our luggage cart herded us into the elevator. "Whatever were you thinking?"

"That Jay never would've forgiven me if I'd gone with one of those two," I said.

Allowing for ample time had been wise. Extracting Pam from the British Museum took half a week; extracting her from the National Gallery took the other half. I learned that London required a full two weeks of malingering strictly down to the museums. Jay and I spent a lot of the second week in cafés and parks while Pam indulged her latest hobby, sketching for hours at the Museum of Natural History and the V&A. She was smitten with South Kensington.

"If Daisy ever takes her back," Jay remarked one evening as we occupied a waterside bench in St. James's Park, "she'll have acquired some culture in addition to manners."

"Daisy wouldn't dare," I said, watching young Italian tourists drop rocks off one of the wooden footbridges. "As long as she gets cards at Christmas and Easter, she's fine."

"I suppose so," Jay said, contemplatively watching the ripples circle outward.

"Pam only has two years of high school left. We'll have to start looking at colleges this fall if she wants to get a head start. If not, definitely next fall."

Beneath the brim of his trilby, Jay had a far-off look. He touched my hand between us on the bench, as if startled to find it there. He curled his fingers around mine, realizing we had little to fear when compared to the impassioned display of Mediterranean youthfulness on the bridge.

"The peace and quiet's a relief. Did you imagine it like this?"

"Imagine what? You once claimed I didn't imagine anything."

"You know damn well what—the future, once we had one."

"Raising my criminally negligent cousin's kid is a surprise."

Jay laughed aloud at that. He laughed as often as he smiled these days. Realizing he'd smiled a lot when I first met him but rarely laughed filled me with sadness in retrospect.

"Cody had it right when he took me in," Jay said. "The teen years are rewarding."

"Are you sure?" I asked. "Livestock-based academic pranks notwithstanding?"

Someone tapped our shoulders from behind. Jay choked in surprise, and I jumped out of my skin. Pam had snuck up on us, approaching from the grass instead of the walkway.

"Such a loathsome display," she tutted. Her sketchbook was tucked under her arm.

Jay held my hand up for her to inspect, shaking it in a playful challenge. "Oh, this?"

"Wet socks," Pam groaned, climbing over the bench, wedging herself between us.

"I still don't see the appeal of that particular figure of speech," I admitted, releasing Jay's hand so I could hug her against my side. "So, what did you draw today?"

Pam held the sketchbook just out of my reach. "Uncle Jay first."

"I *understand* what it means to be a wet sock, you see," Jay said.

"How vulgar," I retorted and almost got shoved off the bench.

"Don't be angry with me," Pam said, surrendering her sketchbook to Jay, "but I've decided I like it here too much. Oxford won't be such a hardship, seeing as it's a day trip, but Ireland and Scotland will just have to wait. I hope they won't be *too* put out."

"They'll manage," Jay said, admiring one of Pam's life drawings of tourists. "If you're not keen on Oxford, just Nick and I could go for a few days. Mind holding down the fort?"

"Please, Uncle Nick," Pam said, pleading before I could voice my reservations. "I can handle it. I was running around Manhattan alone while I was at Spence!"

"As long as you don't mind us calling you twice a week," I sighed.

"We wouldn't be gone a week," Jay corrected. "Just a few days."

Pam rolled her eyes at both of us. "You *could* go for a week."

"It's not as if we'll be sightseeing," I said, and Jay turned pink.

◆ ▽ ◆

I didn't feel like mentioning to Pam that we *did* intend to do some sightseeing. It would've been more embarrassing to admit that Jay hadn't succeeded in showing me much of Oxford outside the Old Parsonage the first time we were there. The morning after our chat with Pam in St. James's, we bade her farewell over breakfast, packed enough clothes for a few nights, and hired a car to whisk us away. The ride was much shorter than I recalled.

We inquired at the Parsonage and discovered no rooms were available.

"There's always the Eastgate," I said before we could even walk away.

Jay was about to say something, but the dour concierge beat him to it.

"The Eastgate's haunted. Unless you like that sort of thing."

I'll tell you what sort of thing we like, I thought with spite.

"Unless you can find us a room by tonight," Jay said, "that's just where we'll go." He removed cash from his pocket and set it on the counter. "Would you mind holding our bags?"

The concierge nodded to where we could set them. "Name, in case something opens up?"

"Carraway," I said and then spelled it for her. "Carraway and Gatz," I added hastily.

"Read a book by some Carraway," muttered the concierge, vanishing into the back.

We managed to restrain our laughter until we were out in the street. Jay took my arm and folded it over his, apparently unconcerned with such a minor impropriety.

"Where can we walk from here?" I asked, enjoying that the choice was out of my hands.

"Everywhere worth walking," Jay replied. "It's not what you'd call a sprawling town."

We crossed Banbury Road like that, arm in arm, without anyone paying us the slightest bit of mind. Instead of taking the next side street, Jay had us cut across the devastatingly picturesque quad of Keble College. I faintly remembered seeing those buildings in the middle distance on our first visit, although nothing rivaled being this close to the stately arches and spires. Jay informed me it wasn't even the oldest of the colleges, having been founded in the late nineteenth century. When I asked him what passed for *old* in a place like this, I'd fully expected to hear something along the lines of the fifteen or sixteen hundreds.

"University College, where I studied a little while, was founded around 1250," Jay said, half-smiling. "There's this ongoing argument between University, Merton, and Balliol, you see."

I marveled over how tranquil his nostalgia now seemed. "An argument regarding which is oldest, or a mundane squabble nobody's been able to solve for centuries?"

"Both," Jay said, hurrying me along the gravel walkway. "I want to show you the Bodleian and the Rad Cam while we're still sober—that is, if I can still find them."

Much to Jay's chagrin, we got lost twice. I helped him save face by asking both times, although neither of the young, hapless locals seemed to begrudge us needing the assistance. The Bodleian wasn't much to sneeze at from the outside, but I was sorry Pam wasn't there to gawk at the exterior of the world's most famous library. Jay was pleased that I found the Radcliffe Camera aesthetically pleasing. He'd always found it so, too, even if he'd never been inside.

Hunger drove us from the Rad Cam's underground bookshop in search of a pub, of which there were many. Jay couldn't speak to the quality of food in any of them anymore, which I found a hilarious statement given that common American folklore held them all to be wretched.

Jay pronounced the fare we ordered at the Jericho passable. I argued that it was actually rather good, but the combination of intoxication and not having eaten since London likely skewed my opinion in the wrong direction. Two ciders for a lightweight like me, Jay said, was two ciders too many, especially when we didn't have a room confirmed anywhere. I didn't have a leg to stand on, as Jay had only one drink and didn't wobble the moment we got up to leave.

"You did that just so I'd have to hold you up, didn't you, old sport?" Jay asked, maneuvering me back in the direction of Keble with an arm tight around my waist.

"Would've entailed knowing th'effects of English cider versus Norman," I slurred.

"Oh, Norman's worse," Jay sighed, patting my hip. "You were a wreck in France."

"Which time?" I demanded, stumbling along only by the grace of Jay's assistance.

Jay snorted and, with great daring, pecked my cheek. "There was a difference?"

I was in no shape that night for notions of romance, although Jay did sweet talk us into a room at the Parsonage that had been vacated two hours before. There was only one bed in it.

"S'pose that's paus—*plausible* deniability," I said as Jay dumped me on the mattress.

"I take back my initial diagnosis," he sighed, flopping beside me. "You're worse now."

"Better than last time," I murmured with an effort, gazing up as he leaned over me.

"I'd take two beds any day," Jay said intently, "if it meant getting to keep you."

"You get one bed *and* me," I replied foggily, stroking his arm. "Where's Pam?"

"I love you to no end, old sport," Jay whispered, kissing my forehead. "I'll call her."

Ever the gentleman, Jay let me sleep late the next morning. I had a splitting headache that wasn't quite a hangover, so he dragged me to the shower with him and then back to bed. An hour and several paracetamol later, it was noon, and the most I felt like was an ass.

"If yesterday was too embarrassing, I'm sure Pam will help you toss me in the Thames when we get back," I said into the pile of pillows. "Maybe it is time I sobered up."

"Let's worry about that later," Jay consoled. "Do you think you could eat?"

"As long as it's room service."

"They didn't offer that last time."

"I'm not leaving this room, Jay."

"I spoiled you rotten, didn't I?"

Jay called the concierge while I fell back into a self-pitying doze. When I woke up again, I was alone in the room, although not for all that long. Jay stumbled through the door with his arms full of two covered china plates and an odd assortment of loose silverware.

After we ate our mediocre English breakfasts, Jay teasingly told me that I owed him. He was implying the only form of currency I reasonably had on my person, and that *was* my person.

"You're too good for this," I said, removing my nightshirt. "Run while you still can."

"I'm too old for this," Jay countered, content to watch at first. "There's a difference."

Eventually, I had to haul Jay from the chair onto the bed and undress him. My low-effort striptease must've paid off because he gasped and shivered no matter where I touched him.

I pinned him down with my full weight, breathing against his ear. "Too old for *this*?"

"Stay here for a week with me," Jay said, a brazen challenge, "and you'll find out."

To avoid giving an immediate answer, I kissed him back into the pillows. There were too many of them for my taste, but Jay didn't seem to mind getting smothered. Eventually, I felt bad for being a tease. I stopped trailing my mouth over his skin at random and applied it with intent.

"Hold still," Jay said afterward, flustered in spite of how sated I'd left him. "Let me—"

"*Jay,*" I panted, taking hold of his wrist so he'd keep his hand right where it was.

"I never get to overdo it," Jay said, but he was glad to see me incoherent. "Overdo you."

"You overdid everything else," I laughed after a while, reaching for my cigarette case.

We stayed for five idyllic days, in which we did precious little sightseeing. When we returned to Claridge's in London, Pam was out, but there were white roses waiting in our room.

Fall of Pam's junior year at Girls' Latin was marked by a studiousness that I had only ever seen the times I acted as her tutor out of necessity. Headmaster Hapgood regularly called my office line at the *Globe* to keep me apprised of her progress. Now that Pam had, as he put it, finally buckled down and focused, she excelled in most of her subjects. I always thanked him for his solicitousness, but I couldn't help but think Pam could just have easily told me herself.

"I'd bet this year's raise it's because you're somebody," Tom said, peering in my door.

I looked up from the theater flyers spread on the desk in front of me. "I'm what?"

"Important," Tom said, leaning in my open door with a smirk. "Nick *Carraway.*"

Gathering the flyers into an untidy pile, I rolled my eyes.

"Journalism isn't glamorous."

"No, but your book went pretty far," Tom continued. "What about the other one?"

"My other . . . " I stared at the latest sheaf of pages I'd set beneath the phonebook.

"You're always working on *something*," Tom said. "Secretive about it, too."

"Memoirs and verse," I replied self-deprecatingly. "Nobody likes a poet."

"They like a memoirist," said Tom, sticking his hands in his pockets. He was unfairly handsome but not as handsome as Jay. "What did the Brits make of you a couple of months back?"

I thought of the concierge at the Old Parsonage. "A few of them heard of my work."

"Think you have time for a drink after work?" Tom pressed. "I've been trying long enough. The old ball and chain's starting to believe you're a figment of my diseased mind."

"As long as Amory's onboard," I said, "I'll phone Jay. Where should he meet us?"

"Not Causeway Street," Tom laughed, turning to go. "Green Dragon, if it suits?"

I waited until lunchtime to ring the house. Pam, there to eat leftovers, picked up.

"I think it's grand you're getting a social life," she said. "Is there *really* a pub called that here? Sounds like you smuggled it back from Oxford. I'll tell Jay where to go."

"He isn't there?" I asked, perplexed. "Never mind. If he's on the harbor, he'll stop home to change. Leave a note where he'll find it. On second thought, you'd better leave a few."

"Later, Uncle Nick," Pam said. She hung up against a backdrop of unfamiliar giggling.

I spent the rest of the afternoon wondering who the devil she'd brought to the house. One of her friends from school, I didn't doubt, but she hadn't mentioned any others along the lines of Caroline.

There were a handful of names she mentioned regularly, but none more than the others.

Jay was waiting outside the Green Dragon when Tom and I got there. He wore the flat cap he often favored for casual outings, fetching in a clean set of work clothes.

"Did Pam mention bringing home a friend?" I asked by way of greeting.

"No," Jay said, clapping my back as he eyed Tom. "And you are?"

"Thomas. The last name's too much of a mouthful. Call me Tom."

"The other half of his party's running late," I said, grateful Jay had left one hand between my shoulder blades even as he'd shaken Tom's. "Has Pam talked about anyone new lately?"

"Not that I'm aware," Jay said, his attention finally narrowing in concern. "Why?"

"I called home at lunch," I said. "I could hear someone else in the background."

"Nick's broody as ever," Tom said. "Our entire office knows about the niece."

"Well, maybe you'd understand if you had a ward," Jay said condescendingly and then turned back to me. "Hapgood hasn't mentioned anything on those tiresome calls, has he?"

"Amory, come listen," Tom said, beckoning to someone behind me. "Domestic woes."

Tom's companion didn't look like the voyeuristic type, but he squinted with keen interest as he approached. I had never seen him before. He and Tom made a striking pair.

"Only the usual suspects," I told Jay. "I suppose we'll find out soon enough."

"Has Boswell here been an ass?" Amory asked, offering his hand. "Charmed."

"That nickname's about a hundred years old," Tom protested, appealing to Jay.

I shook Amory's hand. "No more than he is at work. The pleasure's all mine."

"I'm an incorrigible one for nicknames," Jay said. "Aren't I, old sport?"

Drinks went without a hitch. Amory asked polite questions, where Tom asked insolent ones. They balanced each other so roundly that I wondered if Jay and I could compete. Their ease and familiarity suggested longer intimate affiliation than even Jay and I could boast.

When Jay and I got home, it was late. We lingered in the street, gazing upward. One light burned in the entirety of the house, and it was Pam's bedroom window. Shadows moved within.

"Do you suppose we ought to find out if she's got—"

"Nick, let it go. She'll tell us in the morning, or won't."

When I woke up the next morning, I was alone in bed. The stab of panic I experienced had nothing to do with being alone and *everything* to do with forgetting that it was Saturday. Any other morning, Jay would have seen to it I was awake at a decent hour and out the door. Mildly hungover, I stumbled out of bed, threw my dressing gown on over my pajamas, and carefully made my way down the stairs. Voices reached my ears from the kitchen, echoing clearly.

"He'd worry about practically anything, wouldn't he," Pam was saying, melancholy.

"Not to say that I don't," Jay said reassuringly, over the sound of something frying in the skillet, "but . . . " He exhaled and flipped what sounded like eggs. "Let's say I understand what it's like to have unwarranted scrutiny cast on one's private affairs."

"You must have lived such an interesting life before you met Uncle Nick," Pam said.

Frozen on the bottom stair, I braced both hands against the railing. Jay was dangerously close to inviting questions that he wouldn't want to answer. I held my breath.

"You know I grew up poor. You know I made my way in the world as a jack of all trades for a while. You know I fought in the war and survived. That's about the shape of it."

"I don't know what you were doing in New York. Selling bonds like

Uncle Nick?"

"I was . . . an entrepreneur of sorts, but my colleagues left something to be desired."

"*Oh*," Pam yawned, as if something had dawned on her. "You were a bootlegger."

"That's right," I said, relieved, pretending only to have caught the tail-end as I wandered in. "Fortunately, I swooped in and saved him from an unrepentant life of crime."

"That's awfully shady business, Uncle Jay," Pam fussed, winking at him.

"Which is exactly why I turned back to hard labor," Jay said with forced cheer. He flipped the eggs onto a plate with toast, stepping close as he handed it to me. "*Help*."

"Stocks and bonds aren't what I'd call ethical, either, Uncle Nick," Pam goaded.

"Which is exactly why I turned to journalism," I replied, feeling chipper now that I had a license to be as petty. "Was somebody in your room last night?"

"Why, sure," Pam said innocently. "I was, like always."

Jay's posture went rigid, which meant he was fed up.

"You know what he means, Pam. Answer the question."

"Someone from school came by. We studied late."

"What's her name? When did she leave?" I asked.

"Mara Danvers. None of your business," Pam said.

Jay sagged. "You'd better have locked the door."

"That's the only part that bugs you?" I demanded.

Pam stabbed her eggs until the yolks ran all over.

"You didn't ask what I was up to in London."

"No, but we ought to have," Jay said gruffly.

"I don't sleep with just anyone. I'm not Daddy."

I stared at her while Jay choked on his coffee.

"At least keep us informed of who you're seeing," I suggested, realizing that was the only ground rule we could reasonably set. "Maybe let us meet her?"

Pam glanced at Jay, who was leaning against the stove, and then at me, suddenly calmer.

"Is this how you'd behave if it was a boy? If it ever *is* a boy?"

I considered that while Jay did, reaching my conclusion sooner.

"Nobody's getting anybody pregnant in any direction, so . . . yes."

Pam whistled, relieved. "Thanks for not being sexist about it."

Jay looked like he regretted falling in with a den of shameless libertines.

"Associated . . . maladies and such don't discriminate," he finally said.

Pam rolled her eyes at him. "I told you, I don't sleep with just *anybody*."

"Can we get back to having breakfast?" Jay asked, directing it at me.

"Yes," I said, heaping eggs onto my toast. "What *did* you do in London?"

After Christmas break, Pam woke up to the realization that we hadn't done much in the way of discussing colleges, which was absurd given that was one of the things we'd talked about back when we first met her. She spent January so fixated on contacting schools to request brochures that the coffee and kitchen tables were covered in them by March. Having my desk at work constantly covered in flyers and newsprint was trying enough.

"You won't have time to apply to all of these," I said, impatient.

Pam looked up from her lapful of weekend reading assignments.

"I'd rather be spoiled for choice," she said. "I'm narrowing down."

"I wanted to apply to ten schools. My father and uncles advised five."

"What about your mother and aunts? Did any of them get degrees?"

"No," I admitted. "I regret not knowing what their opinions—well, not true. Aunt Meredith had opinions about everything, contrary. When Dad said Yale, she said Princeton. When Dad said Princeton was better than nothing, she said Harvard. There was a row."

"Perish the thought if somebody mentioned Brown!"

"I was annoyed at all of them, so I only applied to Yale and Northwestern," I admitted reluctantly, joining her on the sofa. "Fortunately, I got into both."

"Drama! Did you regret picking Yale?" Pam asked eagerly.

"Not at first, but your father should've been an early warning sign."

"Daddy alone would've been dreadful, but you put up with a bunch?"

"Your father hung out with medical students who left something to be . . . "

I stopped, realizing why I might regret telling her about that, but it was too late. Pam's teasing expression had shifted into a quizzical demeanor that was even a touch troubled.

"I'd beat them up for you, Uncle Nick, but they're scattered to the winds."

"That's just it; they were never cruel to me. They would've bullied others."

Pam made a face. "You were a spy even back then! What did you see?"

The boathouse incident, it seemed, was about to demand its reckoning.

"The med school cronies had an unsavory idea of fun, Pam. I experienced it once and never spent time with them again. It was when I started spending less time with your father."

Pam rested her elbow on the arm of the sofa. "This is getting sordid. Do tell."

I stared at my hands in my lap, tracing the early signs of age with critical eyes.

"If it weren't for the way they acted toward certain case studies in their textbooks, I wouldn't have been as well prepared to accept you just as you are. I might not have been able to accept myself, either—or Jay. I don't necessarily believe everything happens for a reason, but I believe we can learn from what we observe as much as from our mistakes."

Pam blinked. "Does that mean they were compassionate to folks like us and set a good example? Somehow I doubt it, given they were friends of Daddy's, and you disapproved."

I shook my head. "They would've tormented me had they known I found your father attractive. That was a short-lived infatuation; the more I learned about his character."

"That's boys disgusted by boys who like boys. What does this have to do with *me*?"

In my foolishness, I hadn't shared with Pam the entirety of what I'd learned from Daisy that day on the phone. And I wouldn't have understood all of it if not for that textbook.

"They made fun of a medical chart belonging to a person like you," I said cautiously.

"Jackasses," Pam said, almost dismissively. "It's their job to know girls sometimes turn out like me, even if it's rare. The nurse at Spence was kind, but it's easier for women."

Nodding, I considered my next move. I owed Pam the truth. Her mother had owed it to her, more than just *something's wrong*, but hadn't even been able to follow through. I'd taken the chance away from Daisy, even though I knew she never would've come clean.

"Your mother was going to have that doctor operate on you to see if you really are like that patient chart I saw at Yale. It doesn't *matter* because it doesn't fundamentally affect your quality of life. There are different things that could cause you to develop differently."

"Uncle Nicky," Pam whispered, sitting forward. "What was it about *that chart*?"

"You know about the basics of chromosomal biology," I said slowly, realizing words mattered more than ever. "You know which combination gets associated with which gender."

"Right. So I can infer from what you're saying, and from what I *kind of* know about myself, that XX doesn't always guarantee a womb. Barren is barren. I don't care now."

"Pam, the reason you don't have one is that you might well be XY."

Pam opened her mouth, jaw working, and then snapped it. "What else?"

"All I know is that something related to hormones does the rest— the difference of development on the outside. But you might have other internal differences, too."

Pam looked down at her hands. "You're saying I was meant to be a boy?"

"I don't think it's that straightforward. Maybe you would have been under different circumstances, and . . . " I thought about other kinds of people that those medical students would have mocked, ones for whom the difference was said to be in the mind. "And maybe you wouldn't. Maybe you would even decide that's what you are *now*, learning this."

Pam snapped her head up, fixing me with a steady gaze. "Does Jay know?"

"He knows what you know, only what can be guessed without surgery," I said, consumed with guilt and regret. "It took me a long time to reason through what I found in the archives at work, although I wanted to understand it in case I ever had to tell you."

"What constitutes *has to*?" Pam asked with more sadness than anger.

"Your health coming in jeopardy," I said with conviction. "*Only* that."

Pam nodded, chewing her lip. I could see the gears turning in her head.

"That's not guaranteed to happen, is it? Does science know enough?"

"Most doctors don't ask the patients what they want. Mistakes get made. You were too young and scared. I couldn't believe your parents would risk your safety to find out."

Pam's expression softened, even though she was tearful. She took my hand.

"I can't be too mad. You were only looking out for me like you always do."

"It doesn't excuse my silence. Not telling you was patronizing. I'm sorry."

"You know Mother only cared about how a defect in me would reflect on her and Daddy," Pam said sardonically. "Their high society image. God! They're just *rotten!*"

"If you want surgery to find out, you're old enough now," I told her, resigned. "You graduate next year. Jay and I would worry for you, but it would be your prerogative."

Pam wiped her nose on the back of her hand and then threw her arms around me.

"Hell no! I'd end up in one of those textbooks for shithead Yale boys to laugh at!"

"I don't care who you are or who you become," I said. "That's for you to decide."

That evening, getting home late from the windswept Harbor, Jay removed his hat as he strode into the kitchen. He washed his hands and joined me at the table, leaning to kiss me over the leftovers. He asked how long I expected having to wait on Pam, as he was famished.

"I don't think she's coming downstairs," I said. "She needed time alone."

"With you getting on her case about applications, I can't say I'm surprised."

"Jay, it's not about that. I made . . . well, all right. I made a *different* mistake."

"Don't be too hard on yourself. She's the only kid we've ever raised, after all."

I rubbed my face with both hands. "It's about what her parents tried to do."

"The surgery? That was ages ago," Jay said consolingly. "You spared her."

"Not really," I sighed. "I never told her I figured out what they might've found."

Jay gave me a piercing look, but it wasn't unkind. "You feel guilty about that?"

"I never told you about it. Might've helped if I'd told you first," I said miserably.

"Nick, I'm not ignorant of what can happen out there in the world. I wondered, too."

"That means a lot," I said, "but I'm going to tell you anyway if that's all right?"

Jay tapped the edge of my plate. "Far be it for me to stop you, but you need to eat."

Invigorated by the bracing chill, I turned my back on Lake Waban and looked on this tableau instead: Pam in elegant black poplin and heels with Jay, clad in new-season Savile Row, on her arm. Fresh fall sunlight gilded it—the sundial, the flagstones. All we'd been through with Pam's applications, from mid-spring through summer's end, had brought us to this moment.

"Another pagan holiday, and here we are together again," said Pam. "How vulgar."

By now, that was a favorite in-joke and regular catchphrase between the three of us.

"We would have gone to Normandy if not for this interview of yours," Jay teased while I stood some distance ahead, already at the foot of Tower Court's stone stairs.

"I feel those old bats in the admissions office are suitably impressed," said Pam, moving slowly down the stairs more on account of her shoes than for Jay's benefit. "They ought to be. I'm at the top of my class; those incriminating disciplinary marks be damned."

"You look great here," I said, grinning madly up at her. "It's meant to be."

"This school has a fine rowing team," Jay said, indicating the magnificent view I'd been considering only moments before. "You ought to try out for it."

Pam let go of his hand and descended the last few stairs, almost tripping in her hurry. She grabbed my arm and turned me back toward the water, indicating the well-beaten path.

"They say if you stroll three times around the lake with a fellow, you'll marry him," she said, "so I'd better not walk with you. Uncle Jay, what do you think?"

"I'd better take Nick for a long walk," Jay said, accepting me from her as graciously as a groom might his bride. "As for legalities, we'll worry about that later."

"Maybe they'd do it in Montréal," suggested Pam, winking. "Now, you crazy kids run along. I've got to find those girls I met earlier. We're going to lunch in town."

"Meet us at the train station at seven, do you understand?" Jay said.

Pam appealed to me with a mock pout, but I shook my head sternly.

"I can just stay over with one of them in the dorms! Admissions will be none the wiser, and I'll be home by mid-afternoon tomorrow."

"You're due back at school on Friday," I reminded her with reluctance. "Winter finals are looming on the horizon. It would be unwise to skip now. Ask Hapgood. Think of how hard you worked on your application to this place. Think of your interview."

Only thirty minutes out of it, that was very likely all Pam *could* think of.

"You're as stuffy as Daddy says you were at Yale," she said. "Old bookworm."

"Don't let him fool you," Jay said. "Years ago, he was anything but. He came to my New York parties all the time, and there was one morning back in the summer of twenty-two, before he and I met, when I looked out my window and saw—"

"That's enough," I said hastily, shoving my hands in my pockets as I started along the path. The last thing I needed was for Pam to start asking questions about what she thought of as Jay's bootlegging days. "Corrupt her with lies as much as you like. Treat the girls to lunch, for all I care. It's too nice a day to sit inside. I'm walking."

"You sound so much like Mother when you talk like that," said Pam, wistfully.

"Look here, dear heart," Jay said, nudging her back toward the stairs. "Go. Stuffy old Nick will be all right. I'll see to it he doesn't fall in the lake and drown."

Pam paused at the top of the stairs and waved back at us, her countenance as radiant as arriving October. She blew one kiss, a second, a third—and then, hobbling out of shoes that dangled magically at her wrists a moment later, she was gone.

"Things being what they are," I said contentedly, taking Jay's offered arm, "she'll get in."

"Buchanan's not a name to be trifled with anywhere in the Ivy Leagues," Jay replied.

"That's not what I meant," I sighed, but I knew that what he'd just said was the truth.

"Of course not, Nick. Her brilliance puts yours to shame, but—still. Meet me halfway?"

"Fine. Pam's wealth has opened every door she's ever strolled through—except ours."

Jay fell silent at that, mulling it over for a long time as we walked the shimmering shore.

"She accepted some obscurity," he said at length, "leaving home to come live with us."

I thought about the checks Daisy sent at regular intervals—tuition, travel, birthdays, holidays—wrapped in blank stationery. Pam sent cards, but her parents never wrote back. I wondered if it would go on like that forever—if Pam would simply wake up one morning to find herself an heiress with no idea what her parents thought of the woman she'd become.

"Do you think they'll come when she graduates from Girls' Latin next summer?" I asked.

"The real question is if she wants them to," Jay replied. "If she decides to invite them."

A cluster of mallard ducks darted out of the undergrowth, crossing in front of us before flapping down the embankment and into the shallows. We paused to watch that tiny family feed, splash, and complain to each other. Happenstance often proved maddeningly heavy-handed.

"I never want to see them again," I said. "For Pam, though, I'd grin and bear it."

Jay set his hand at the small of my back, urging me on. "I'd bear it for you both."

"It's got to be her decision. I won't be guilty of taking another one out of her hands."

"Could be that I'm biased, but I don't think you ever took from her as much as you helped prepare her for the ones she would face. None of them were going to be easy."

"I sheltered her," I said and then realized how self-centered my statements were. "No—we did. That's something we did together, even though I might've led the way."

"We protected her. Sometimes you've got to do that for people you love."

I stared at the bend in the trail ahead and then across the water. There was a stately white residence, just large enough to be considered a mansion, at the far end of the lake. My first thought was to wonder if it was part of the college and, if so, who lived in it. My second thought was that I wanted it for us—to be closer to Pam, in the event this was where she ended up.

"Penny for your thoughts?" Jay asked, startling me out of my reverie. "What is it?"

"That house," I said, pointing. "I don't remember reading about it on the map."

"Hunnewell Estate," Jay murmured. "Not part of campus. Just borders on the lake."

"If it's ever for sale, I want it," I said. "Maybe we can afford it by the time we retire."

Jay stopped in his tracks, spinning me to face him. "Nick, we already have a house."

I stepped closer to him than I had ever dared in public, emboldened by the stillness.

"This is what you've made of me, Jay. I want to be the one to give *you* everything."

"You already have, old sport," Jay said, taking my face in both hands. "Count on it."

New Year's Eve 1938 was the most frigid I could remember since childhood. All evening, my thoughts circled back and back to the dreamlike tranquility of that first and only trip to Saint Paul that Jay and I had taken together. Meanwhile, in one tastefully illuminated brownstone among many on Pinckney Street, our party was in full swing.

"You Yale boys are all the same!" Amory shouted from his vantage point on the dining room table, Perrier-Jouët in hand. He waved it at me in accusation. "Even your evening dress smacks of the country club—ain't it so, Boswell?" he appealed to Tom.

"Never more than now, my dear Johnson," Tom said. It was gratifying to see him scandalized by Amory's behavior, unable to seize the spotlight. "For Christ's sake, get *down*."

"I can't even remember how to golf!" I shouted to Amory. "You'll have to teach me!"

Tom seized my arm with a fearful look of warning. "Don't encourage him, Nick."

I shrugged and left with my half-filled champagne flute in hand, working against the crowd to find my way back to the sitting room. We'd held our first New Year's bash the year after I started at the *Globe*. It had been the highlight of my co-workers' calendar ever since.

Next to the piano, Jay was still engaged in conversation with my boss, Taylor, who ardently wanted Jay to renovate *his* yacht after seeing what a bang-up job he'd done on ours. I caught Jay's eye, nodded, and turned to find out who'd stumbled elbow-first into my back.

It was Taylor's wife, Miranda, already deep in her cups. She was being inexpertly waltzed around the floor by a starry-eyed copy editor from advertising.

Finding my glass empty, for I had been sipping on it the entire time, I briefly contemplated shoving my way back into the dining room to join Amory on the table. This idea was fortuitously killed in its cradle by the doorbell's abrupt, insistent chime.

"Stay there," I said to Jay on my way past the piano. "I'll see who it is."

I found Pam glittering from hair to ankle on the front stairs, and beside her, a devastatingly attractive young woman with dark skin and even darker eyes. Pam had mentioned Sylvie Saint-Germain on her rushed weekend visits home, but those had been few and far between. She was enjoying her second year of college immensely.

"You took the train all the way from Wellesley on a night like this?" I asked incredulously. "Surely there's a Tower Court party you're missing out on."

"Rumor has it there's a pair of over-the-hill Princeton boys here who love to drink," Pam said glibly, stepping up to kiss my right cheek, "but that they're really only interested in each other, which is a shame," and then my left. "Any thoughts on our prospects?"

"One of them is on the dining room table," I said, offering Pam's companion my hand. "You're welcome to him." Sylvie took hold of my hand, and I brought her knuckles up to my lips. "You must be Miss Saint-Germain. Any friend of Pam's is a guest of honor."

"Pam says you made her turn in too early last year," Sylvie murmured. "So, all things being equal, in addition to being a year older, we decided we'd just turn up."

"That's sensible," I told her, stepping back to hold the door. "Come in, ladies, come in! Most drinks are in the kitchen, so help yourselves. If you want Perrier-Jouët, fight Amory for it."

To the best of my recollection, Sylvie's aristocratic New Orleans Creole mother had defiantly, happily wed far below her station to an immigrant Swiss cobbler. I thought of Tom Buchanan's inevitable apoplexy at this family history and was marvelously comforted.

Pam had already found Jay and was hanging off his neck like she hadn't seen him in months—which, to be fair, she hadn't. We'd been begging her to come home since early November. I hovered nearby to overhear Sylvie's introduction, which went as most first introductions to Jay tend to go—which is to say, *memorably.*

Never once was he anything but Gatsby in my eyes at these soirées, rendering that erstwhile incarnation's rarity so much the richer. Since neither of us was much for Halloween, I told him it was the one time of year he was welcome to risk giving himself away.

Pam left Sylvie with Jay, who wasted no time in making Sylvie the sole point of focus in his immediate orbit. Meanwhile, Pam came over to stand beside me with two Sobranies perched between her lips. She lit them both with a single drag and then handed one to me.

"Mother was in love with Jay once, wasn't she, Uncle Nick?" she asked in a low, incisive tone, disturbing my reverie. "She was in love with him, and you stole him away."

Speechless, I hesitated for a few seconds. Jay glanced my way and smiled.

"That . . . actually, yes, that's about the shape of it," I said. "The short version."

"You'll have to tell me the long version one of these days," she said, producing a gold-plated cigarette case from her clutch, which she sprung open right under my nose. "I found some interesting newspaper clippings in the basement of Clapp Library, dated 1922."

"Is that so," I said with caution, gratefully taking a spare smoke to stick behind my ear.

"You are the cleverest, insanest man alive," Pam whispered, dropping the case back in her clutch. "If you're the one who manipulated the New York press with just a few comments—which, courtesy of my research, I think you *are*—then I wonder why you didn't seize on what that Wilson woman's sister said and see to it Mother ended up behind bars."

Several puffs on my cigarette later, I was dizzy, supported only by Pam's hands at my elbows. This wasn't how I had imagined the confrontation, if it ever happened, would go.

"Because of you," I said. "I let it go for the simple fact that you *existed*."

If Jay wondered why Pam was hanging tearfully on *my* neck by the time he and Sylvie decided to join us, he had enough courtesy and restraint not to ask. I transferred Pam over to a bewildered Sylvie and begged for a moment alone with Jay.

We made our way upstairs to the library, which had fortunately been vacated by whichever couple had most lately taken sanctuary there. As an unspoken rule, if the door was locked, it was wise not to stand there knocking for too long.

"She's put two and two together," I said, securing the door behind us. I tested the doorknob just to make sure it wouldn't budge. "She knows who you are, and she knows what her mother did. She wanted to know why I didn't see Daisy hang for it."

"I hope she's grateful," Jay said. "Her life would've been much worse if you had."

"Well, she's in tears just now," I said, leaning against the spine-lined shelves that passed for a wall. "There's suspecting something, and there's getting confirmation."

"Maybe she read your editorial on what's happening in Europe, old sport," Jay suggested, helping himself to what was left of my cigarette. "This Hitler situation's got an awful lot of people on edge," he said uneasily, puffing it down to nothing. "She might be afraid Uncle Sam will send us packing again. She may not realize we're too old now."

"Fuck," I said. "I hadn't even thought of that. She's probably worried sick."

I started toward the door, but Jay set a hand on my shoulder, holding me in place.

"I miss these nights," he said. "I dream of it sometimes. The entire house is a glorious, shimmering crowd, but the only face I can see in the midst of it is yours."

"Then let's add May Day and Midsummer to the rota," I suggested, only half-joking.

Jay leaned close, pinning me against the reassuring solidity of bound, printed matter.

"It's times like this that I wish I hadn't been so blind right at the start," he said, one finger tracing an imaginary line from just beneath my ear down to my collarbone, his thumb deftly loosening both bowtie and buttons on the way. "No, blind's not the word I'm looking for. I watched you from the first moment I saw you because I liked looking at you. What I mean to say is, if I hadn't been so set on Daisy, so goddamn deep in *denial*—"

"Shut up, Jay," I said tipsily. "Don't think I didn't know. You insisting that I ought to use your beach as often as I liked was honestly the last straw. Did you enjoy the view?"

"If I told you what I thought about while I watched you, Nick—what I *did*—"

"God," I said, heedless of just how much of my clothing he'd removed. "Do."

"Told myself it was better than thinking of anyone else," Jay murmured. "Safer."

"Now you're getting colder," I teased. "Nobody likes to be a poor substitute."

"You weren't," Jay said, shirt and trousers undone. "I just didn't know it."

There was a certain nervous difficulty to the first few minutes of our rushed trysts, always, what with raucous glee drifting up from downstairs and nothing else to lean against but books. The desk was annoyingly small, but I ended up there flat on my back with all four limbs wrapped around Jay. I heard the frantic trill of an improvised scherzo on the piano downstairs.

Thomas Parke D'Invilliers had once mentioned at the office that he could play, but he'd neglected to specify he was just shy of a virtuoso. Amory Blaine would have elaborated on that theme had he been present, I supposed deliriously, pressing my mouth against Jay's skin.

Delightful that Jay was halfway to spent when I'd done nothing but kiss his cheek.

"Stay right where you are," I gasped, already lost. "Goddamn it, Jay. Don't *move*."

We'd managed to clean up just to the point where our collars needed tending when the door miraculously unlocked itself with a momentous, unannounced *click*. Jay and I stared at the befuddled young women in the doorway, one of whom had the key from the top drawer of our bedside table dangling from her wrist by its threadbare blue satin ribbon.

"Gosh, I'm sorry," Pam said, offering me the key as if in apology. "You shouldn't have shown me where you kept it if you didn't mean for me to ever actually *use—*"

"It's fine," I sighed, accepting the key. "Don't mention it. You're bored?"

Pam exchanged sheepish looks with Jay while Sylvie studied the shelves.

"Those friends of yours from the office made a fake show of coming on strong. Sure, I made a joke about them on my way in, but do you think I'd even *kiss* somebody who went to Princeton? We couldn't hear ourselves think over the piano, so I thought we'd come up here."

"Room's free," Jay said, restoring his bowtie with practiced ease. "It's all yours."

Sylvie turned away from the shelves, chuckling in delight at our dishevelment.

"Sweetie, is that why you brought me all the way to the city?" she asked Pam. "To show me that even your stuffy old uncles are down with Boston marriage? I already knew *that*," she said and leaned in to kiss the corner of Pam's rouged lips. "Sure, I'll shack up with you on Charles Street someday, but aren't our rooms in Severance Hall good enough for now?"

"Ugh," Pam sighed. "Yes, as long as we've got a couple of years left. I *suppose*."

"I know your daddy would pay for it in a tick, but I love the view we've got."

"You can see the courtyard?" I asked while Jay neatly reconfigured my collar.

"Even better, Mr. Carraway," said Sylvie. "We've got clear sights on the green."

"Then you must be in one of those turret suites," Jay said with instant admiration.

"Why don't you show me where you sleep when you're home?" Sylvie asked Pam.

"We'd better get back downstairs," I lamented halfheartedly. "We've been bad hosts."

"Never, Uncle Nick," Pam said. "Not you, either, *Gatsby*," she told Jay, winking.

They left us standing alone in the library with the door hanging wide open.

"Did we do the right thing, taking her in?" Jay asked as the music resumed.

"It was your idea in the first place," I reminded him. "May I have this dance?"

Every year, as befitted tradition, there were a few people who turned up to our parties unannounced. Pam and Sylvie were the most welcome of these, followed by various grown children, relatives, and other miscellaneous hangers-on associated with my co-workers. The copy-editor from advertising wasn't yet known to me, although he would be if he lasted.

Year in and year out, there was one visitor I'd hope for, peering suspiciously out of the corner of my eye as Tom monopolized the piano or as Jay and I shared a dance. If the crowd was around a hundred at its height, then I convinced myself there was a good chance I'd spot someone who at least resembled the one thrill-seeker I most longed to discover lurking.

I regretted that I had never asked for the name of the one person whose company was there when I needed it most. He hadn't struck me as a young man at the time, so there was distant awareness on my part that, if he was still alive, his partying days were likely behind him.

For a long while, Jay and I were lonely men. We had always done our best to surround ourselves with a simulacrum of friends. For me, it had been Tom and his enclave of uncouth medical students in the boathouse at Yale, and eventually Jordan. For Jay, it had been a series of unfortunate entanglements beginning with Cody and ending with Wolfsheim.

Later that night, after the drinking, dalliances, and dancing, I inspected the house to make sure everyone had gone home. Behind Pam's door, she and Sylvie were asleep.

When I joined Jay, he was waiting with the covers turned down.

"No sign of Klipspringer, then?" he teased, tugging me into bed.

"Why would there be? It's Owl-Eyes I was looking for," I said.

CHAPTER 7

Breathing Dreams

Ever since first meeting Sylvie at New Year's, Jay and I had impressed upon Pam repeatedly that we wanted to spend more time getting to know her. We knew the girls hadn't lacked the desire to come and visit, but their time was at a premium. I would never have imagined that English and biology majors were similar degrees of constantly tied up.

When they finally came to stay over spring break in March 1938, they brought news concerning the one extracurricular pursuit they seemed to have in common: Shakespeare Society. Pam's sense of drama had been inherited from Daisy—and, dare I say it, even a fraction from long exposure to me. That had been Jay's tongue-in-cheek assertion; Pam had spent too much time listening to me wax excessively poetic over the Bard. I was unrepentant.

What they had brought with them was a cast list, presumably copied from the master document hung on a door somewhere in the memorable miniature sixteenth-century style house on campus. Distantly, I recalled strolling by it on the day we had taken Pam for her interview and tour. To think that a mere visual landmark of several years before was now a place in which Pam spent a significant portion of her after class hours was sentimentally satisfying.

"Well, go on," I said. "I won't eat a bite till you tell us who got what."

Jay cleared his throat and took my glass away from me, nodding curtly.

"Best to get it over with, good news or bad. We're proud regardless."

"The cast list wasn't supposed to be up till after break," Pam explained through a mouthful of key lime pie. She'd commandeered her dessert for eating first, in spite of Sylvie's backside stinging gesture of protest. Daisy had arranged by telephone for the confection to be sent up from Pam's favorite New York bakery in the wake of her weekend trip there with girls from school. They'd neglected to bring some back themselves.

"Instead, Jacqui typed up enough copies for everybody, rejects included. She had her stage manager shove them under our dorm doors at three in the morning. We argued about the list the whole way up here," said Sylvie. She took a crinkled piece of paper out of her lap, glancing conspiratorially at Pam. "The train conductor wanted to kick us off in Hartford."

"Let's see," I said, plucking the piece of paper from Sylvie's offered grasp. "*Hamlet*, to be presented by Wellesley Shakespeare Society in April, date to be announced, directed by Jacqueline Broadhead—that may bode ill, I suppose, if she lives up to her name—and . . . "

I trailed off, reaching for my glass. This time, Jay leaned over my shoulder to read the creased list instead of trying to prevent my continued indulgence. I perceived mild shock as Jay's breathing changed. I hadn't expected what was typed there any more than he had.

"You didn't mention auditioning for the lead," Jay said. "We thought you two read for Rosencrantz and Guildenstern. There was an understanding that your studies come first."

"We *did* read for supporting roles!" Pam protested. "Honest! Jacqui has a bent sense of humor." She picked up her wine and swilled it, eyes rolling up to scrutinize the ceiling. "I get all the lines," she said, taking a swallow, "and Sylvie gets the emotional onus."

"Horatio's lines are nothing to sneeze at," Sylvie told Pam, stealing a bite of her pie. "And I'd like to see *you* try leading Isabel around that stage when she's full-on mad Ophelia."

Bad enough without casting lovers in the relationship that's really at the heart of the play, I thought, but kept my mouth shut. I raised my glass to them instead.

Jay clinked his glass against mine and then against Sylvie's and

Pam's. In spite of his protests, he must feel it a celebratory occasion indeed to permit himself a drink.

"Congratulations are in order, but I don't want you getting too stressed before finals," Jay said, sounding guiltier with each misgiving. "Promise us you'll pace yourselves."

"That might not be possible," Pam said. "Jacqui has some odd ideas."

I raised an eyebrow, my head already swimming. "What are those?"

"She wants to rehearse from the end," said Sylvie. "Work backward."

"Might be a sound way to go about it," Jay replied. "An old friend of mine used to say you should start where the rope's most tangled. That final scene is as tangled as it gets."

I glanced at him, half-smiling. "I didn't know you had opinions on Shakespeare."

Pam threw one of her gloves at me; Sylvie restrained her from throwing the other.

"I have opinions on a great many more things than when we first met," Jay said to me, setting the paper down, and then looked at the girls. "What is there to argue about?"

"Jacqui thinks we'll be too soft with each other," Pam scoffed. "She told us to, I quote, *go home and do some research.* That was awfully cagey. Before you ask, she knows about us. What's the difference, whether it's love between men, or love between women or love between anything else? It all looks the same to *me.* She must've meant something different."

"Oh, I know what she meant," I replied. "Did you tell her about *us?*"

Pam blinked, but Sylvie's expression indicated that she'd caught on.

"I told her we were going to my uncle's place in the city," said Pam. "Why?"

"A lot of folks on campus have *Globe* subscriptions just because of Nick's column, sweetie," Sylvie said. "Stop pretending you don't know. More than half of *those* have society parents on the East Coast rumor mill. They read his novels, too. See where this is going?"

Fed up with the conundrum, Pam made a courageous effort to finish her drink. In the wake of Sylvie's question, which hung expectantly on the air between them, Pam set her glass down too sharply. Red wine splashed vivid, bloody violet across her cheek.

"Fine. So Wacky Jacqui is honorable enough not to want us to get found out."

"We just need to be as manly as possible. Then there's no way it's not an act."

"Then you've got to read it for us," Pam concluded, wiping her cheek.

"The entire play?" Jay jibed uncomfortably. "Let's at least eat first."

"Not the whole thing," Sylvie said. "The offending article. The *scene*."

I refuse to be sober for this, I thought and drained the rest of my glass.

Dinner proceeded as a quiet, plate-scraping affair with the pie devoured first and the main course scantily touched. We finished the first bottle of wine and, to my approval and Jay's frustration, Pam went to fetch another from the cellar. I wanted to argue that I hadn't put a portion of my wages toward building a modest yet refined selection of the grape for naught.

"For the road," Pam quipped, hefting one dusty bottle over each shoulder as she returned to the dining room. She set them down on the table and then pointed the corkscrew at Jay's nose. "You're reading Horatio, and he's," she indicated to me with a jerk of her chin, "reading your sweet prince. We can't have this resembling life too closely. Objections?"

Let me count the ways, I thought but stood up somewhat unsteadily and offered Jay my arm. "If hearing it read out loud will help you with your rehearsals, I see no harm," I lied, leading everyone into the sitting room. "Only the part that's relevant, though."

I was glad not to have to drag my copy of the *Complete Works* down off the library shelf upstairs; both of the girls had brought home their digest-sized reading copies of the play. They situated themselves on the Chesterfield, full glasses of wine in hand, while Jay and I knelt on the rug and frowned at the thoroughly annotated books we'd been handed.

"Do we just . . . start?" Jay murmured, flipping pages to the end. "*Where?*"

"He is justly served," said Pam, affecting her voice so as to make Laertes sound noble yet enfeebled. "It is a poison tempered by himself. Exchange forgiveness with me, noble Hamlet. Mine and my father's death come not upon thee, nor thine on me."

I scooted down so that I lay half on the rug and half across Jay's lap, feeling my age in the process. I held up my book so that it didn't clash with Jay's and, tapping Jay's wrist with one corner of the front cover, whispered, "Laertes just died. That's our cue."

Jay moved his book aside, the better to scrutinize my face. The disquiet and vague confusion there, at least, meant Jay didn't have to fake any of his performance. Even though I hadn't participated in stage drama since my Yale days, I could work with that.

"Heaven make thee free of it!" I called earnestly in Pam's direction.

I let the dizziness of sinking back down in Jay's lap serve as a foil to Jay's arms closing around me in alarm, his book awkwardly dangling. I'd done this scene once at Yale as part of a variety show; only we'd really hammed things up—titular pun most *definitely* intended, at least at the time. The words flooded back to me unbidden, if somewhat corrupted by time and intoxication. I dropped *my* book, as well as the lines that I'd always felt were superfluous.

"I follow thee. I am dead, Horatio. You that look pale and tremble at this chance, had I but time—oh, I could tell you," I touched Jay's cheek, "but let it be. Horatio, I am dead. Thou livest. Report me and my cause—"

Jay's sudden, ragged breath startled me into silence. He let his own book drop harmlessly to the rug, a quick study out of long years' habit. His tears fell from above, several in succession, dashed like wine—*like rain*, I thought, pushing the memory away—across my cheek.

"Never believe it," Jay said, frantically glancing down at his open book, his performance entirely too convincing for any soul present. "I am more of an antique Roman than a Dane. Here's yet some liquor left . . . " Casting wildly about, he reached for the closest wine glass on the coffee table, never mind whose it was, snagging it with shaking fingers.

One of the girls took a stuttering breath and held it. Under any other circumstances, I would have known which of them it was, but my field of vision had narrowed to Jay's memory-fueled anguish. I wondered how often he had taken a moment to imagine what those frantic minutes after finding him shot had been like or the hours I'd spent in Huntington Hospital at his side. The wine had only increased the intensity of my initial maudlin misgivings.

"Give me the cup!" I demanded urgently, finding I didn't need to feign difficulty breathing. "Let go! By heaven, I'll have it," I continued, prying the glass away from him, and drank it down. Jay gaped, all tears and outrage, but I forged on, letting the glass fall. "Good Horatio, what a wounded name shall live behind me. If thou didst ever hold me in thy heart—"

I couldn't have prevented Jay from kissing me at that moment even if I'd wanted to, and I *didn't*. Throughout the decided conclusion of our performance, we received applause from Sylvie and whistling from Pam. Eventually, I was short of breath again, so Jay eased off.

"I have to say, though," Pam remarked as Jay and I helped each other to our feet, "that was pretty damn soft. Maybe we've got to invite Jacqui here to prove our point."

"No way," Sylvie said, fetching both her wine glass and Pam's. "Let's leave your poor old uncles alone. They need some time out, looks like."

The girls retreated upstairs, leaving us alone in the middle of the sitting room. Jay sat down on the sofa where Pam had been sitting moments before, reaching for the glass that might previously have been mine. He drank with an urgency I tended to associate with myself.

"Bereft over Hamlet and Horatio," Jay muttered. "I see what you mean, old sport."

"What I mean?" I echoed, sinking down beside him, the words distantly familiar.

"That first day back," Jay prompted. "After Huntington deemed me fit to discharge."

I nodded, unsurprised that I should have mentioned it so early in our involvement. It took a few seconds of maundering through recollections for me to pinpoint the precise moment.

"No, it was the day after *that*. We spent the night before trying not to injure you further."

Jay cracked a wan smile. "You did admirably, all things considered. A true gentleman."

"You understand now," I said. "Why I was thinking of that in particular, I mean."

"If it had been you, I would've been torn up to no end. But I wasn't thinking along those lines at the time. I'm sorry for it. My stubbornness was what put us in that situation."

"Don't worry. Also, there's something else. When you said the wounded name line, I thought . . . *well*. Not a thought, more of a feeling. What you had to leave behind."

"Gatsby's no wounded name," Jay said. "Not anymore, no small thanks to you."

Gratefully, I leaned against his shoulder and decided against refilling my glass. Jay's patience with both the girls and me throughout the evening had been exemplary. If he still regarded himself as essentially selfish, then Pam and I needed to work toward disabusing him of that notion. He had, over the course of time, become irrevocably selfless.

"I think we've switched places in more ways than one," I muttered.

"No, no," Jay protested, turning my face toward him with still unsteady fingers. "If you mean . . . " He hesitated, the second glass catching up to him. "What do you mean?"

"You lost your selfishness, and I found it. That's not a favorable reversal, Jay."

"Give yourself some credit. Your selfishness is your own, but . . .

it's hardly the first quality that comes to mind. You'd do anything for me, *anything* for Pam and Sylvie."

Shaking my head, I leaned into him harder. "You're the only ones I'd do it for."

Jay shrugged, resting his cheek against the top of my head as if he saw no issue.

"They say family ought to be like that. You and I never had that until now. Family worth doing anything for. Why, I used to believe it was just fantasy. Stuff of fairytales."

"You're drunk," I told him. "How often do I get to be the one to say that?"

Once *Hamlet* had run its triumphant course and classes had let out for the summer, Sylvie invited Pam home to New Orleans to meet her family. This announcement manifested as a jarring change of plans. I had previously arranged for Pam to spend June, July, and August interning at the *Globe*. Even Jay's hopes were dashed, as he had hoped she might spend her weekends with him out on the Boston Harbor. Pam was put out at having let us both down but not to a sufficient degree that she was willing to tell her paramour she couldn't make it.

"Anyway, I don't see the problem," Pam said, helping me water the rows of herb seedlings we'd cultivated on my usual typing table in the greenhouse. "It wasn't a paid internship. Since you didn't budget for sending me off, I'll just . . . " She squared her shoulders. "I'll call Mother and tell her I need tuition for a summer class. She'll be none the wiser."

I pointed so Pam would realize that she had absentmindedly flooded the pots of rosemary. She had a lot on her mind; I didn't blame her, but I was frustrated.

"Something tells me Daisy will know that's not what you intend to use it for. Three months in New Orleans costs a damn sight more than a three-credit language course."

"I can always tell her it's a travel practicum. Sylvie and her family speak Creole, French, and German. That's on top of English. You know from firsthand experience my French needs work. I was abysmal that time we were in Paris. Nobody understood a word."

"There's a difference between Parisian French and Louisiana French," I said. "Guess which your mother would expect you to learn, and guess which you'd actually learn?"

"That's classist," Pam said with reproach, setting down the watering can. "You know Sylvie's mother's family is rich. And her father might have started out poor, but he *did* come to this country from Switzerland. For all you know, his French is as proper as his German."

"How do you know he doesn't speak Italian and Romansh instead?" I asked, scooping mucky soil back into the affected pots. "Swiss German is different from—"

"I'm going, Uncle Nick," Pam said stubbornly, brushing off her hands. "You can't change my mind. You haven't spoken to Mother in four years, and I know you don't want me to, either. That's why I said I'll take care of it. You and Uncle Jay needn't worry."

"No, but we will anyway," I sighed. "What if we travel down with you?"

Pam beamed, knowing full well she had me right where she wanted me.

"Oh, Sylvie will appreciate it so much! You can meet her family, too."

"What's so urgent all of a sudden?" I asked, sensing an unseen variable.

"Europe is practically at war. Her father's beside himself with worry."

"Switzerland isn't involved. Her relatives are as safe as they can be."

"Nowhere in Europe is safe for Jews right now! Don't you read the news?"

"Touché, but . . . wait. I thought Sylvie's father was a protestant. Saint-Germain?"

Pam was looking at me with a shade of the expression she often wore when she was thinking about or talking about her father. It was the furthest thing from reassuring.

"Sylvie's middle name is Shana, after her paternal grandmother. Shoshana Koch."

At that point in the conversation, I felt like a heel. Pam had always been particularly skilled at exposing my blind spots. I hadn't known that Sylvie's father was Jewish. I peeled off my gardening gloves and set them aside, penitent under the weight of her gaze.

"I should know not to make assumptions. You hate it when people make assumptions about us, and here I am, making assumptions about others. I'm sorry."

Pam gave a curt nod, apparently satisfied, peeling off her own filthy gloves.

"We're welcome to arrive a week from now, but a fortnight would be polite."

Jay must have caught the end of the sentence as he wandered into the greenhouse. He carried an assortment of pastel-shaded macarons on a plate, more suited to spring than the swiftly oncoming summer. Ecstatic, Pam went to him right away and claimed several.

"A fortnight for what?" Jay asked warily, offering the plate to me next.

"Change of plans," I said. "We're going to New Orleans next week."

"Two weeks from now is fine," Pam reminded me, her mouth full.

"New Orleans," Jay repeated, struggling to catch up. "Sylvie?"

"Her family invited Pam," I replied, "and us by extension."

"We have an awful lot going on here at home, old sport."

"Sylvie's family has a lot going on. Relatives overseas."

Jay helped himself to the last few macarons, considering.

"The Swiss side of the family ought to be safer than . . . "

Pam's withering expression halted his train of thought.

"They're at risk, Uncle Jay. A very *particular* risk."

"Oh," Jay said apologetically. "I hadn't thought. I see."

"It's been stressful. They'd appreciate the company."

"I only wish we could do more to help, dear heart."

"The distraction will have to be enough," Pam said.

On Monday, I was stuck with the unenviable task of explaining to Taylor that he'd be losing not only a promising summer intern but also *me* for a month or more. When I proposed an arrangement in which I'd compose and mail my columns on the strictest deadlines I could manage, his skepticism relented by a fraction. Finally, he assented.

Word of my audacity got around to Tom, who wasted no time in coming to grace my office with his insolent presence after our mid-afternoon staff meeting. He loitered, smirking.

"La Nouvelle-Orléans. Nearly as bad as naming yours truly. Have you ever been?"

"No," I said, shuffling papers in the hope he might leave. "Jay has, I believe."

"Back in his illustrious cabin boy days with Captain Cody, I would gather?"

I scowled at him, disliking the implication. "If you're going to be rude—"

Tom dropped the glib façade, contrite. "We'll be in a pinch without you."

"I've worked out an arrangement with Taylor," I said. "It's all in hand."

"Famous last words," Tom said morosely. "Dear Amory will be beside himself if we lack for your fine company at the Dragon. Do you promise to send Mardi Gras postcards?"

"Mardi Gras is over," I said, feeling sorry for his and Amory's clear lack of recourse to adventure. "We'll send whatever postcards we can find. Would streetcars and gardens suit?"

"Maybe one of those miniature maps with overblown landmarks, a gator or two."

I returned his affably jealous grin, saluting. "I'll do my utmost, dear Boswell."

"The last straw!" Tom wailed. He threw his flat cap at me and walked away.

When I told Jay and Pam about the incident over dinner, they spent the entire evening proposing appalling postcard designs. I told them we weren't likely to find even half of those imaginary horrors, which Pam took as an affront. She pulled out her sketchbook and got to work.

The night before we left, I took great satisfaction in leaving the first home-drawn, water-colored piece of correspondence on Tom's desk. It featured a parade of cartoonish alligators in Mardi Gras beads. On the reverse, Pam had scrawled, TO MESSRS. BOSWELL & JOHNSON WITH REGARDS, CAN'T SPELL OR FIT THE REST. WISH YOU WERE HERE.

Pam's sense of humor had been apparent to me from the first time I heard her voice over the phone, although such trifling manifestations as that postcard and the NEXT WEEK'S RAG paperweight she'd made for me were the exemplars I treasured most. She might make a fine humorist if she put her mind to cultivating the impulse at greater length.

When Pam confessed that she wanted us to make the journey by train instead of driving, Jay threw his hands in the air and said the logistics would be none of his concern. Fortunately, I knew from intermittent travel for work that if he'd tolerate the *Columbus and Cincinnati Express* from Boston to Saint Louis, we could then take the *Chickasaw* line directly from there to New Orleans. All told, it would add up to a week and a half of travel, which Pam declared perfect.

"It's been forever since we took a trip!" Pam exclaimed, enchanted as we boarded the *Express*. "I, for one, am in no mood for those stuffy ocean liners. Look at how quaint these sleepers are! You two have been just dying for a dose of honeymoon nostalgia. *Perfect.*"

We left Pam and her tiresome effusiveness to their own devices during that first three-day leg of the journey. We stayed in our sleeper with the blinds drawn, too tired from the whirlwind of packing and arranging for responsible parties to look in on the house in our absence—none other than Amory and Tom. I told Jay I regretted not knowing where Magda was.

"Was this how we got to Saint Paul back in the day, old sport?" Jay asked, ruffling my hair as we smoked and lounged to the tracks' constant, lulling rhythm.

"No, it was the *Chicago Special*," I murmured drowsily, stubbing my cigarette out.

"I dare say you're the one to blame for my romantic impression of travel by rail."

"Nonsense. You traveled Europe by train long before we ever decided to . . . "

Jay was regarding me with the most peculiar, reverent fondness I had ever seen.

"I'm glad we decided to," he said with emotion. "More than you'll ever know."

"Where's that marriage I was promised when we walked around the lake?"

"The best I can do is second, third, fourth, fifth, and sixth honeymoons."

"Seventh," I said, pitching his cigarette. "Wait—sixth is right if we count—"

"I don't know what counts anymore," Jay admitted, pulling me against him.

Spending an intimate, balmy afternoon in borrowed linens had become a delicacy, and we reveled in it. That evening when I dressed and went out to the dining car to fetch provisions, Pam gave me a mock scandalized look from where she was eating alone at one of the booths.

"Never act your age," she said to me as I swayed back through the car, winking.

The second leg of our journey was longer, a week in and of itself, and required more variety of diversions. Jay taught Pam how to play the card games he'd previously felt she was too young for, chiefly ones oriented toward riverboat gambling. I had misgivings but quickly realized it was absurd to fear for Pam if she was on the arm of a seasoned practitioner.

"Don't worry, Sylvie never counts cards," Pam reassured me. "What does it matter to her if she loses twenty dollars here, fifty dollars there, a hundred? What does it matter to *me*?"

"Ain't we got fun," I sighed, staring out the window as Jay shuffled the deck.

"Haven't heard that song since I was small," Pam said. "Mother loved it."

"You should ask Nick to sing," Jay said. "He's got a decent voice."

"Arrange for orchestral backup, and then we'll talk," I demurred.

New Orleans in June was one of the muggiest localities I had ever experienced. Not even a week of breathing Louisville air could rival the lungfuls of swamp I had swallowed on our streetcar from the station to Sylvie's ancestral home in the Garden District. By the time we reached the mansion's broad, immaculate front stairs, Jay and I were both dripping with sweat.

Pam looked cool and collected, as was her right. She rang the bell.

Instead of a butler, it was Sylvie who opened the heavy oak doors.

"You're all a sight for sore eyes," she said, kissing Pam's cheek.

"You, too, my dearest," Pam said, embracing Sylvie with care.

Jay and I removed our hats, bowing before the girls led us inside.

Calista and Auguste Saint-Germain gave us a welcome that put the Buchanans' long ago attempts at high hospitality to shame. All throughout lunch, they fawned over the girls and asked avid questions about what Jay did for a living up north. It struck me as strange that there were no such questions about my profession, although that matter was soon demystified during dessert.

The butler, wherever he had been while we ate, brought in a modest, tidy stack of *Boston Globe* back issues and set them at Calista's elbow. She set one deliberate, diamond-adorned brown hand on them and said, "Mr. Carraway, you must tell me which of these to read first."

I was happy to recommend a few, but I couldn't in good conscience claim she should read *all* of them. Auguste leaned over, whispering that I ought not to indulge her too far.

When our kind hosts impressed upon us that we must stay under their roof as the girls intended to do, I thanked them and apologetically explained that Jay and I had already secured lodgings in the French Quarter. As dusk fell, Jay and I trundled back onto a streetcar with our bags and crept toward the twinkling heart of a city that slept more seldom than Manhattan.

Our balconied rooms above Royal Street were in view of the Cathédral Saint-Louis, furnished lavishly in a style that not even Jay could name. While we unpacked and bickered about what to do with ourselves for the duration of our stay, revelers carried on. I made Jay vow that he would impose moderation on me if I succumbed to Bourbon Street's temptations.

It didn't take long for me to realize that the promises I'd made to Taylor were not feasible to keep, not when Jay realized that New Orleans presented an entire port-of-call filled with untainted memories for us to share. I sent a telegram to Tom, asking him to take over my column for the foreseeable. He wrote back with feigned disdain, but I sensed his unfettered delight.

I had no way of knowing when, precisely, Pam had found the time to speak with Daisy or by what means—but the expenses she'd paid on our behalf were exorbitant. The sum of money that I discovered in my account on phoning our bank the next day suggested that Pam had never had any intention of us returning to New England a day sooner than August's end.

<hr />

Our return to Boston was delayed until the first week of September. Jay and I left New Orleans fat, happy, and without Pam in tow. Calista had reassured us that both girls would arrive in Massachusetts just in time for fall convocation. Rail travel felt like less of a guilty indulgence now that we were beholden to no one but ourselves again, but I worried about Pam anyway.

In our two-and-a-half-month absence, Tom had kept both the house and my column in tip-top shape. Taylor threatened to outright replace me with Mr. Parke D'Invilliers if I so much as run off for that long ever again. With Pam's benevolent, ever-increasing financial influence over our lives, I couldn't help but wonder if that promise, too, was one I could not reasonably keep.

Pam sent a telegram when she and Sylvie set out from New Orleans for Wellesley. Jay called it the better part of valor that the girls hadn't informed us that it was an unsupervised road trip in a Cadillac Series 60 newly gifted to them by Auguste. I asked Jay if he was jealous of the vehicle, to which he demanded, incredulously, if the yacht wasn't good enough for me.

For whatever reason, her increased devotion to Sylvie notwithstanding, Pam came home nearly every weekend. When I asked her if it meant their relationship was in peril, she told me not to be ridiculous. She cited the fact that Sylvie got to have her during the week, and so why *shouldn't* she devote more time to her uncles? I pretended to grumble about it, secretly touched, but Jay was unabashedly over the moon. He took Pam sailing at every opportunity.

In the days immediately following our return, Jay's client list doubled. His absence for most of the summer had left his current projects in stasis. Boats, mercifully, may wait regardless of their condition—but the mortals to whom they belong frequently know no such patience. Harried, Jay doubled down on his restoration work. This resulted in longer, later hours on the Harbor that made me afraid for his health. Pam's increased presence was a comfort in these circumstances, as her assistance to him on weekends was far more valuable than any internship at the *Globe* would have been to Taylor and me combined.

On September 16, news of a tropical cyclone in the Atlantic hit our weather desk, sending a concerned murmur throughout the rest of the publication. That evening, I asked Jay if there had been any disturbances on the Harbor and if he would consider packing it in until the storm had dissipated. Jay didn't respond immediately, which concerned me.

Since it was Friday, Pam had come home in time to eat dinner with us.

"Don't fuss, Uncle Nick," she said. "It'll blow out by the time it hits the Bahamas."

"Maybe, but you still wouldn't want to be there when that happens," Jay remarked.

"That's not far off," I said. "Not when it comes to a two-hundred-mile-wide storm."

"More like three or four hundred," Jay said. "You've got to respect that much power."

Pam looked unsettled. "If it doesn't blow out, could it reach the coastal South?"

Jay shrugged. "It could reach anywhere on the East Coast if it doesn't die down."

"All the more reason to avoid the waterfront for the next week, maybe?" I asked.

Jay looked up, his demeanor heavy, which suggested he'd heard me the first time.

"I don't think I can stay away for that long," he said wistfully. "Jobs to finish."

Uncomfortably, Pam glanced rapidly back and forth between the two of us.

"I'll go out with him every day," she told me. "I won't go back to school till the storm's gone. They'll understand if some of us stay home while there's a risk of high winds and rain."

"As long as you're sure, I'd appreciate the extra hands," Jay said before I could protest.

I didn't see Pam and Jay until late on both Saturday and Sunday nights. They came home in filthy work boots and denim overalls, exhausted but satisfied with everything they'd accomplished. Jay came to bed with reassurances of manageable wind and waves. Monday at work was blessedly quiet; Jay and Pam got home early enough for family dinner.

"Pam, I want you to stay home tomorrow," Jay said over coffee after we'd eaten.

"That's ridiculous!" Pam protested. "We're making good time catching you up!"

"Nick hasn't seen enough of you," Jay said with an edge to his voice. "Stay home."

"Jeez Louise, *fine*," Pam retorted. "I can tidy up and cook while he's at work."

"I'd appreciate the help and the company," I admitted. "We can catch a movie at the nickelodeon when I get home. I've heard good things about *You Can't Take It With You*."

"That would be nice," Pam said, genuinely contrite. "Sorry I've been neglectful."

"I appreciate it," Jay said. "Somebody's got to take care of him when I can't."

I studied Jay's face in profile as he finished his coffee, touched, but puzzled.

"Sometimes I think there's a conspiracy between the two of you," I sighed.

The next morning, our weather desk was abuzz with talk of New Jersey and Long Island. I had too much to do leading up to about four o'clock, but every time I heard voices in passing, they ran the gamut from uneasy to frantic. I finally left my desk and peered into the hall.

"What *about* New Jersey and Long Island?" I asked when I saw Tom approach.

"Storm's hit 'em," Tom said grimly. "There goes the Atlantic City of my youth."

Alarmed, I spun on my heel and went to my office window, which, down to a misfortune of desk and chair arrangement, spent all its time behind my back. I was met with an overcast, threatening sky and trees roiling in the wind. I stood frozen, but my heart raced.

"Nick?" Tom tried, tapping me ineffectually on the shoulder. "Old sport?"

"If Taylor asks, I went to check on my niece," I said, shoving past him without even taking time to close and lock the door. "And if that's a problem, you're welcome to my job!"

Pam was standing in the back garden when I got home, in her work clothes and one of Jay's old flat caps. Even though it had begun to spit rain, she was motionless, her arms folded across her chest. She was staring at the sky with an inscrutable single-mindedness.

"Are you all right?" I asked, finding I had to raise my voice above the wind.

"I've got a bad feeling about why Uncle Jay told me to stay home," Pam said.

"Me too," I agreed, setting a hand on her shoulder. "We'd better get inside."

Pam shook her head, agitation finally evident. "No. It'll be bucketing soon."

"All the more reason!" I shouted as it began to pour, and thunder split the sky.

"We should've told *him* to stay home," Pam said bitterly, grabbing my arm, dragging me back inside. She didn't stop when we reached the kitchen. "Where are the raincoats?"

"Cellar," I said, breathless, understanding what she was on about. "I'll get them."

In galoshes and rain gear, we fought our way downhill against the freezing onslaught to Cambridge Street. We flagged down the only cab we could find, which wasn't difficult given the driver had been idling on the curb, staring through his windscreen at the terrifying sky.

"Waterfront," he repeated, as if he couldn't comprehend Pam's request. "You joking?"

"No!" Pam shouted, shoving me into the back seat. She handed him what looked like about forty dollars from her pocket. "I'll make it a hundred if you want! Go!"

The streets were empty enough of cars that we got there in half an hour. Three blocks from the water was as close as the driver would leave us. I got a firsthand demonstration of Pam's formidable sprint—and learned just how incapable I was, in my increasing middle age, of keeping up. She finally backtracked and grabbed my hand, virtually dragging me to the pier.

"The one we've been working on is docked here!" Pam shouted, leaving me at the foot of the slick wooden stairs as gusts buffeted and shoved us. "See it there?"

"Yes!" I shouted, staring at the yacht, which had begun to pitch on the water and then stared up the stairs at her. "Pam, be careful! Do you think—"

"I'll go grab Uncle Jay!" Pam shouted down at me and then tore off down the pier.

Before I could think better of the action, my sheer, unadulterated terror had begun to propel me up the stairs. I only made it halfway before someone grabbed the back of my coat, yanking me back down with such force that I fell into their arms. We toppled into the silt.

"Nick, what in God's *name*—!" Jay shouted, wild-eyed under his hood. He tightened his hand at the back of my neck, crushing our heads together. "You ought to be home with Pam!"

My breath died in my throat. "She's up there," I choked. "On the pier, she went to—"

"Jesus *Christ*, now you're really wet socks!" Pam yelled down at us. "I'm just *fine*!"

"Get down from there! *Now*!" Jay roared, his voice raw with emotion, but he wasn't looking at her. He held me so close, so tight that not even a storm surge could have torn us apart.

"Jay, we found you safe," I said, freezing and soaked to the bone. "Let's go home."

The journey back was unpleasant, with few cabs available. Since the T had shut down, we had to hail three separate drivers just to make it back to Beacon Hill. Never at any point in that miserable, sopping wet hour did Jay release my hand for more than a heartbeat.

Once we were dry, with all limbs accounted for, Pam made us tea, mumbled her apologies on delivery of the tray, and hurried upstairs. When I called after her, insisting we weren't angry, she shouted back—it wasn't that at all, she needed to phone Sylvie!

Jay stared at the flames in the grate for a while, huddled against my side beneath the oversized wool blanket Pam had fetched for us. He shivered miserably.

"I should've listened to you. Should've shut it down. Stayed home."

"I'm not angry at you, either, Jay. But I was worried sick, I admit."

Jay seized me by the back of the neck again, dragging me forward into a kiss. We carried on while the storm raged—tangled and tearful, far too relieved to even pause for breath.

As the months passed, we followed the progress of Europe's war, which was now in earnest, determinedly finishing our breakfast morning after morning. As bombs fell on Wieluń and Rotterdam and Turin, the remainder of Pam's third and beginning of her fourth year at Wellesley passed without incident. She came home most weekends, lest we should vanish while she wasn't looking—sometimes alone, but more often than not with Sylvie at her side.

Daisy came to stay with us from Christmas 1940 until New Year's 1941, which surprised me, given the rocks on which we'd foundered for a while. Pam and Sylvie were on track to graduate in June, which made me realize with distress that her parents would likely be attending commencement. Jay, with that air of calm, long-suffering acceptance he'd cultivated, reminded me that sanctioning their presence was Pam's prerogative. Our burden was to tolerate it.

The ceremony and all of its attendant festivities were held on a sweltering afternoon that, at least in climate, reminded me of nothing so much as the ill-fated day on which we'd all piled into Tom's coupé and Jay's Kissel and had let our irritable mutual hatred do the rest.

We'd seen Pam off with her classmates earlier that morning, leaving them to their robing and their lineup, before taking our seats inside the vast tent with its dignified platform stage and podium. The tent had filled with a steady, gradual hum, and I doubt I would have noticed the Buchanans' arrival if not for Daisy's unbidden laughter several rows ahead of us.

"Tom hasn't aged well, has he, old sport?" Jay asked in a low, satisfied tone.

I nodded in agreement, nonetheless too displeased to speak. Some part of me had been hoping he'd find it in his heart to stay away, but even I knew the measure of affection he rightly bore for his daughter. Thicker about the middle and possessed of a woefully thinning pate, he coughed his way through Karl Taylor Compton's dignified address. We might have remained under Tom's radar for a little while longer if not for the fact that we, like Tom and Daisy, rose to applaud with raucous enthusiasm when Pam crossed the stage.

That surreptitious glance over his shoulder was the first time in nineteen years he'd set eyes on me—and, come to think of it, the first time in nineteen years he'd set eyes on Jay. The moment was worth replaying in my mind's eye, if only for the depth of Tom's astonished distaste at the sheer, affable cheek of Jay's warmly offered smile and wave.

"He'll murder us afterward over champagne and cocktails," I said under my breath, my eyes fixed on the stage while all of us applauded. "So much for civility."

Pam blew two hurried kisses, grabbed her diploma, and, shoeless, dashed across.

"I don't think so. Not on his little girl's big day," Jay said. "He wouldn't dare."

In the reception tent afterward, a moment I'd long been anticipating had finally found us.

"You've got to swallow your pride and say hello," said Pam, dragging me along on one arm while Sylvie occupied the other. "Daddy will play nice. I made him promise."

Jay followed close behind us, stiff and formal, not entirely immune to nerves after all.

"Mr. Carraway," Tom said, taking my hand in his grasp, clapping my arm hard enough to leave a bruise. "You're looking well after all this time. Pammy's been taking good care of you, has she?" His eyes flicked over my shoulder, coming to rest on Jay's features.

"No, don't be ridiculous," Pam said. "That's Jay's job. You know him, don't you?"

"Mr. Gatsby," sighed Tom, heavily, reaching past me to afford Jay only the curtest, briefest of handshakes. "Or whatever you've got people calling you these days."

Sylvie smirked but schooled her features quickly when Pam elbowed her.

"It's a pleasure to see you again," Jay said, "under such auspicious circumstances."

"Tom may read big words, but that statement's a stretch," said Daisy under her breath, for my ears only. We'd reached an uneasy truce, and, in circumstances like these, blood tended to prove thicker than sweat. She fanned herself uneasily.

"Daddy, this is Miss Saint-Germain," Pam said, presenting him with Sylvie's hand, which she'd taken delicately in her own. "Mother met her at Christmastime."

Tom blinked at the woman next to his daughter as if seeing her for the first time.

"Congratulations," he said, taking hold of her hand for the briefest of moments before unceremoniously releasing it without a kiss. "Very liberal-minded, these people up here."

Pam's fury was fierce, sudden, arm looped through Sylvie's quick as a snake-strike.

"Honored, I'm sure, Mr. Buchanan," Sylvie said, latching onto Pam just as tightly.

"Sylvie's a scientist," Pam said coolly. "Do you understand what that means, Daddy?"

"Against all odds, it means she's got a better chance at a paycheck than you do."

"I don't know," I told him, satisfied by the ferocious shade of red he'd turned. "Journalism's reliable, and there are more and more women in the business yearly."

"I've read your books," Tom said, his focus falling on me, as I'd hoped it would. "They're too short. Not much happens in them. Why don't you just write poetry?"

Oh, I do, I wanted to tell him, but it's not for public consumption. Instead, I valiantly ignored Jay's knowing quirk of a grin and said, "The critics certainly seem to appreciate my brevity. If I went on any longer, they'd never compliment me again."

"You're not intellectual enough," said Daisy, winking. "You've got too much heart."

"I'd rather have his heart than a head full of nonsense," said Sylvie, yawning. "Sweetie, we'd better get out of here before too long. We've got a train to catch."

"Pam says you're going out of town for the weekend," said Daisy, looking me in the eye. "All four of you. Something by way of a graduation present?"

"We promised Pam a trip out to Long Island," Jay said before I could respond, and I was grateful for the intervention. "She'd like to see our old stomping grounds."

"Good luck finding anything worth the trip," Tom scoffed. "It's stomped to bits." With that, he set a hand on his daughter's shoulder and kissed her forehead. "I'm proud of you, baby girl. Be careful running around with these people—do you hear me?"

"I'm one of these people," Pam said. "Uncle Nick's full of stories. I want to see them."

"You will," Jay told her. "Wonders upon wonders. Nobody else can show them better."

As the girls dashed off to find Sylvie's parents, the four of us stood drinking in silence.

We'd booked rooms at the Garden City Hotel from that evening through to Sunday, which made it more of a week's getaway than just a weekend jaunt. Pam and Sylvie spent the first twenty-four hours shut up against all comers, which was just as well, given how much rest Jay and I needed now between bouts of our own exertions.

"They're worse than we were in Montréal," I said, resting my forehead against Jay's cheek. "Didn't think it was possible." I found his scar with my fingertip, circling it.

"They'll have to come out tomorrow morning, whether they like it or not," Jay said, shifting fully onto his back so I could sprawl on top of him. "We've arranged for the car to West Egg, and there's no rescheduling it." He arched appreciatively in response.

"We might've been worse on the ship," I said, kissing his neck. "Or on the train."

"Far as I'm concerned, you're twice as bad now," Jay said, so I rewarded him for it.

At ten o'clock the next morning, we waited patiently outside the girls' door with several empty bottles for company—two Louis Roederer Cristal and one Château d'Yquem, both 1922 vintages. Tom and Daisy must have given Pam a staggering sum for graduation.

The girls emerged looking elegant and collected, if languorously weary. They kissed us good morning and asked if we'd slept well. We both agreed that we had.

"Let's see this legendary old neighborhood," said Pam, yawning behind her left hand.

Something winked there in the hallway's low light, glittering cold stones in a white gold or platinum setting. The delicate band of diamonds was Tiffany, at a guess, and I wondered if the fortune belonging to Sylvie's heiress mother was to blame.

"Not without hot breakfast," said Sylvie, beckoning us down the hall. "My treat."

"We've only got an hour till the car arrives," I reminded them. "We'd better hurry."

"No, the driver had better *wait*," Sylvie replied, "given what I'm willing to pay him!"

From start to finish, breakfast in the hotel restaurant only took forty minutes. The girls' demeanor was much improved once they'd eaten, although I'd seen Pam with a hangover sufficiently often to know she was still feeling the previous two nights' revels. Our hired driver was a stoic sort who didn't speak much. Combined with the girls' sound dozing, Jay's pensive silence, and my self-contained misgivings, the ride was eerily quiet.

Just as the taxi pulled up in front of my run-down former residence, Jay glanced back at me from the front seat. I shook Pam, whose head had lolled onto my shoulder.

"We're here," I said, "or what passes for it, at least. You'd better wake Sylvie."

Sleepy amazement held us there in the neatly swept lane, an unearthly silence settling as the car drove away. The tiny cottage was only slightly more run-down than I remembered it, the unkept walkway and trimmed white roses on the trellis meager signs of present habitation.

Pam led the way around the cottage's periphery, determined. Her sturdy work boots, the ones she wore to the waterfront with Jay, left prints in the rain-softened, uncut grass.

Sylvie stepped past Jay and me, catching Pam's elbow. "What do you see?"

"Mother wasn't lying," Pam said. "It's a shack, all right, but it's adorable."

I stopped, watching them continue ahead, unable to address Jay's questioning hum.

"We ought to go around the front," I said, "and apologize to the current resident."

"You don't look well, old sport," Jay said, but he followed. "We shouldn't have come."

Before he could catch up, I'd dashed up the front stairs and knocked on the door.

The weathered face of the woman who answered passed from fear into disbelief.

"Mister Nick," she said, disbelieving, her accent worn down by decades. "Is it . . . "

Jay was quick to step in, and with more grace, too, than I could have mustered.

"We're sorry to trouble you, Madame Vehko," he said, hat in hand. "Yes, it's us."

Jay's choice of honorific was filled with humility and tact, what when I'd never known the woman's marital status, let alone her surname. I wondered how he'd discovered it. She embraced me first, and then Jay, an armful of tear-misted Finnish endearments.

"Those pretty ladies in the back—ah, I am happy! They are your wives, surely?"

"No," I said. "The blonde is my niece, Pam, and the other girl's her friend Sylvie."

"Pam is a very tall girl," said Magda approvingly. "Just like Finnish girls. Strong."

"It's absolutely wonderful to see you again," Jay said, smiling. "May we come in?"

For the next hour and a half, all four of us endured strong, unmilked black tea and stale butter cookies at the hands of my former housekeeper. Admittedly, Magda's willingness to chatter saved Jay and me a great deal of explanation-induced fatigue.

"They left me," concluded Magda, finally, on her third cup of tea. "No warning, I tell you, but a note on the table and some money. Fortunately, *very* much money."

I glanced sidelong at Jay, who, lowering his eyes, coughed politely into his hand.

"So it was off to Canada, then?" asked Pam, feigning innocence all for Magda's benefit. "Off to Montréal, Québec City, England, and France. What a time you must have had! Jay told me once that he found traveling romantic, *especially* by train. Was it, Uncle Nick?"

"Why are you asking me? You already have the answers," I said curtly.

"Children are like this," said Magda, turning to Pam. "Europe is always romantic."

"Paris in the springtime, sweetie," said Sylvie. "You've been there. You told me."

"Yes, I have," Pam sighed, slumping down a little in her chair, "but not with *you*."

Magda rose, clearing the tray, which was the same one I'd used to serve Jay and Daisy.

"You must go see the old house, Mister Jay," she said, returning. "It is not the same."

"I expect not," Jay said. "Not since I handed it over to Wolfsheim. Never the same."

"If this is Meyer Wolfsheim you mean, he is dead," Magda replied. "Eleven years gone."

"Who owns the place now?" I asked, too curious to hold my tongue. "Did he sell it?"

Magda shook her head darkly, wringing her wrinkled hands in her tea-stained apron.

"It is for sale," she said. "Always for sale. Rich men come and go but never stay."

Jay nodded gravely in thanks and rose from his seat, his restless eyes on the door.

"We'll go and have a look at it, then," he said. "Show the girls for old times' sake."

"It was beautiful in my day," Magda said. "In Mister Nick's, too, and also in yours."

All of us bade Magda a fond farewell, but she lingered over Jay longest of all. What afternoon conversations they must have had in my work-trapped absence during those six weeks Jay and I had stayed, I couldn't guess, but he had clearly endeared himself to her for the remainder of her days. Moneyed or penniless, that was his way.

The front gate to the adjacent property was padlocked, but that didn't prevent Pam, seasoned boarding school prankster that she was, from picking the lock with a pair of Sylvie's hairpins. We hauled the gates shut behind us.

Pam expertly rewrapped the chain and snapped the lock back in place. I had a sense of distinct foreboding, being shut inside a place from which there was no escape, but the risk of being seen along a private posted stretch of beach—that or the sea. I didn't doubt we could swim for it if necessary, but I didn't relish the thought of returning to our hotel sopping wet.

Sylvie murmured profanities under her breath as we crunched up the gravel drive.

"What kind of a godforsaken eyesore is this place? You white boys are nuts."

"I might've chosen better," Jay admitted, "but it's the location I was after."

None of the locked entrances yielded to Pam's dormitory approach, but, ever resourceful, she found a cellar window that boasted an ominously large crack. She sat down in the grass and shattered what was left of the dusty glass with one swift, exacting kick.

"Ladies first," she said smugly, extending one grass-stained hand to Sylvie.

The interior was a solid murk of dust-moted, humid darkness. Pam and Sylvie vanished down half-remembered corridors, their ghostly laughter echoing off the high ceilings and down to where Jay and I stood in the staircase-wreathed gallery that had once housed his wardrobe and bed. It was empty now, dappled with afternoon sunlight from the shuttered windows high above.

"I almost can't breathe in it, Jay," I said, at a loss. "I still don't know what to say."

"Didn't expect you to say anything, old sport," Jay sighed. "You liked it. Daisy didn't."

"Do you ever wonder what might have happened if we could've stayed here?" I asked, pacing a wide circle from where Jay stood at the heart of it all, the still point's center. "If Wolfsheim taking it all hadn't been the only way. If you could've kept it."

Jay shook his head, hands in his pockets, staring up at the ceiling.

"You were right all along," he said. "We had to leave. Things would've gotten worse."

Sensing his wistfulness, I paced the circuit again, returning to stand as close as I dared.

"I know that's how it would have been," I whispered. "I dream of those nights, too. I see the cars, the crowds. I hear music even now. I wish I'd stayed with you long past sunrise. I never got to use the pool. I might have seen that lunatic coming. I wish I had stayed. I *never—*"

Jay kissed me, and our world hung on the words left unspoken, suspended in that moment. Ripples of might-have-beens lapped at the edges of our fragile universe—absorbed and grounded, made new by Pam's clear-voiced, echoing intrusion from the gallery.

"This place is haunted, Uncle Nick!" she called. "We're going outside! I need air!"

Jay didn't stop kissing me until both sets of footfalls far above us had retreated.

"Let's go find them outside," he said. "A stroll on the beach will calm everyone."

"Wait a minute," I said, halting him. "There's something I always wondered—"

"Of *course* I loved you too," Jay said. "Every moment she was slipping from my grasp, every moment my doubt grew stronger, I loved you both. I know now what she meant by that. She loved *me*, too, but loved Tom more and more with every waking hour. How could I admit to understanding that, Nick, back then with everybody watching?"

"You couldn't," I insisted. "You couldn't have done it, Jay. I don't blame you."

"Good," Jay replied, dragging me by the hand, turning his head as he led us on toward daylight. "Because you meant more than all of this, more than what I couldn't reach."

We emerged misty-eyed to the sun's merciless glare off the waves and to Sylvie pointing urgently toward the water. The dock was as it had always been, the only thing unchanged.

"I told her she'd better not go out there, but she wouldn't listen," said Sylvie. "What if those old timbers have rotted through? Your Pam's a pretty fool. I hope she can swim."

"She can," Jay said, scrambling up the stairs. "In waves much rougher than this, too."

Sylvie helped me up the stairs after Jay. By the time we got to the top, he had already reached the point where concrete gave way to wood, shouting into the wind.

"Pam, whatever you think you're doing out there, you had better . . . " Jay's voice faded at the sight as surely as my own would have done but not in despair.

Pam turned from where she stood at the dock's farthest end to stare back at us, her pale hair ablaze, with blue sky and cirrus clouds and Long Island Sound shimmering beyond her for miles. She extended one sure hand to us—a peace offering, safety, so we went.

I would like to think that our modest boat has done a better job than most of withstanding the inexorable current of year upon year, decade upon decade—but I'm not so arrogant as to believe us immune to the delays of heartache. I've learned by hard example, absorbing those persistent ripples of the past, rendering them null so as to propel us onward, *forward* . . .

And so, dear reader, please promise me this. Should you outlive us, crack open the heart of even *this* ending—and find what must wait patiently for us there.

About the Author

AJ Odasso's poetry, essays, and short stories have appeared in magazines and anthologies since 2005. Their first full poetry collection, *Things Being What They Are*, an earlier version of *The Sting of It*, was shortlisted for the 2017 Sexton Prize. *The Sting of It* was published by Tolsun Books and won Best LGBT in the 2019 New Mexico/Arizona Book Awards.

AJ holds an MFA in Creative Writing (Poetry) from Boston University. Currently a PhD candidate in Rhetoric & Writing at the University of New Mexico, they teach at University of New Mexico and Central New Mexico Community College. They have served as one of the Senior Editors in the Poetry Department at *Strange Horizons* magazine since 2012.

What does an author stand to gain by asking for reader feedback? A lot. In fact, what we can gain is so important in the publishing world that they've coined a catchy name for it. It's called "social proof." And in this age of social media sharing, without social proof, an author may as well be invisible.

So if you've enjoyed *The Pursued and the Pursuing*, please consider giving it some visibility by reviewing it on Amazon or Goodreads. A review doesn't have to be a long critical essay, just a few words expressing your thoughts, which could help potential readers decide whether they would enjoy it, too.

Lightning Source UK Ltd.
Milton Keynes UK
UKHW020649070822
406948UK00008B/877